PROLOGUE
THE FALL OF DOBEHEN

The Cycle 11174
Drakón Standard

Living fire burned in the oils of Nük T'nyr's flesh and the græsteel of his blade. "Kurhri da'm te nurrin var ma'hdden!" belted out the king of the Empyrjurin as he led his armies down from the way-veiled encampments in the highlands.

"Kurhren da'mer se nurrem var ma'hddri," his soldiers shouted out in reply as the ground shook beneath their boots.

A league from the walls of the Alvish city, the dance of war began. His armies clashed with the vanguard of the defenders. The tiny Alvs seemed ill matched against his great warriors, but Nük T'nyr knew from experience not to underestimate the power of the Alvs.

"Estygin ma'hn var der'x gher," he commanded.

His generals relayed the order. His armies dug in.

As predawn twilight began to reveal the landscape, concentric rows of trenches encircled half the city. In front of the trenches, a half-league of rank-and-file defenders stretched back to the city's massive gates.

The war dance continued. The lines of defenders marched on Nük T'nyr's trenches; the entrenched soldiers beat them back. His soldiers poured out of the trenches; the defenders raised shield walls and hurled javelins. Through it all, Nük T'nyr fought alongside his soldiers, greeting the defenders with laughter that boomed and echoed his scorn as he fought the tiny Alvish soldiers.

Just before the yellow sun of the Alvish world rose, Nük T'nyr turned his eyes to the heavens. "Kurhri da'm mo'rren sur umdeh'n," he cried; and his armies prepared for death to rain down. Death came in the form of shadowcraft that left the air tasting of brimstone, smoke, and copper.

The Empyrjurin name for such a shadowcraft storm was *mo'rren te nasci*—a deathstorm. The deathstorm came in the form of rain, wind, and lightning. Slitrain that cut through flesh to the bone. Blackwind that choked and strangled. Shadelightning that struck without warning.

Although the trenches ran with rivers of blood, the survivors were many. They rose up with renewed ferocity, riding waves of will and force, and attacking with the full fury of the Empyrjurin people, purging the fields before them with steel and living flame.

Nük T'nyr's great battle sword ran with blood—blood that sizzled, popped, and smoked in the living fires of the blade. None could stand before him unscathed, and his scorn-filled laughter gave his armies hope.

He did not know doubt, for the Scarabaeid Praefect had blessed

RISE OF THE FALLEN

RUIN MIST: DAWN OF THE AGES

ROBERT STANEK

RISE OF THE FALLEN

RUIN MIST: DAWN OF THE AGES

ISBN: 978-1-57545-097-1

REAGENT PRESS
WWW.REAGENTPRESS.COM

him on the eve of the battle and told him that decisive victory would ensure the Jurin peoples' rise to greatness. He even dared to hope for freedom—he would cut out his own heart to know its taste.

The very thought of freedom drove his arm and his blade. He showed no mercy, gave no sympathy to the fallen. Soon he was standing in the open fields well beyond the trenches, having helped his armies beat back an Alvish rush after the storm.

It troubled him that he could not see the whole of the Alvish city laid out before him. Among his kind he stood a head taller than most, and yet the walls of the Alvish city were raised just beyond the level of his eyes. The closer he approached, the less of the city he could see. Raising one hand in a fist and his great sword in the other, he called out to his crafters.

The Scarabaeid dropped the way veils around the Empyrjurin encampments and marched forth even as the Alvish regrouped and renewed their attacks. Looking down, Nük T'nyr saw two tiny soldiers climbing up his legs, each with a blade in his teeth. Moving swiftly, he clubbed them with the backs of his hands before they could strike, and then ground their flesh and bones into the earth of the field.

"Myuk ngoth d'er," he told the Scarabaeid as they joined him at the front lines.

"Kurhri mo'rren te hurre var de'trod," the Scarabaeid replied as one.

The arrival of the Scarabaeid was followed by the arrival of Nük T'nyr's generals. Kha'el D'erth stood beside his king, drawing himself up, and clutching his shattered coat of mail and the bandages beneath. He hoped he could hold in his guts until the battle was won and he could rest.

In a show of support for the gallant fighting through the night and into the day, Nük T'nyr clasped Kha'el D'erth's shoulder, forming a plan of attack while his generals spoke their reports. His reinforcements were coming up behind the city, from the direction of the rising sun. Their siege weapons and breaching towers were sure to catch the Alvish defenders off guard, for the defenders were focused on attacking his trenches.

Nük T'nyr passed Kha'el D'erth a flask. The general turned the flask up and drank. "Kurhri," Kha'el D'erth grunted, handing the flask back. Nük T'nyr nodded, took a long pull from the flask as well, and passed it along to his right. Ghul Rwern repeated, "Kurhri," and downed the liquid fire.

Afterward Nük T'nyr smiled fiercely at his generals. "When the yellow sun sets we shall rule this city," he said, "I do not intend for this to end otherwise. The Scarabaeid will keep the Alvish shadowcraft in check. Keep your soldiers within their protective cover. Do not let them stray." Then with his two top generals at his side, Nük T'nyr ordered his reinforcements to wage an all-out assault to increase their chances of success, even as the defenders dropped back to regroup in great thousand-member squads before the gates.

Nük T'nyr's features were ablaze as he stalked forward. Flames ran down his arms into his græsteel's blade, which readily drank them in until it glowed red-hot. Fire burst forth, leaping into the air.

As the Empyrjurin began their charge, the Alvish shadowcrafters called blackwind, slitrain, and shadelightning down from the sky. But this only brought a return of Nük T'nyr's scornful laughter. He was ready this time, and his Scarabaeid sundered the storm and turned its ill effects aside.

When the armies clashed, Nük T'nyr found himself in the shadow of the black walls. He cast back his head and called his father's name to the heavens. To fight by night or day, twilight or dawn light, was right; but to fight by shadow was wrong. Every fiber of his being told him so.

"We must reach the gates," he told Kha'el D'erth and Ghul Rwern. "Once we breach them, we can sweep through the city and bring this to a close."

His battle fury turned to rage and he fought on, driving toward the great gates of the city. Kha'el D'erth and Ghul Rwern never left his side, and right behind him was the Scarabaeid Praefect. Together they cut a swath across the Alvish ranks. Kha'el D'erth hardly seemed to feel his wounds, and Ghul Rwern was as untiring as Nük T'nyr himself.

When the Alvish shadowcrafters discovered their magics had no effect, willcrafters were brought forward, for the Alvish were strong in all manner of craft. As the Praefect battled spirit and dream, Nük T'nyr set upon the grotesqueries of air with his græsteel blade. The Alvs seized the opportunity to form new lines and reinforce their place before the gates; so by the time the Praefect and other Scarabaeid vanquished the spirit demons, Nük T'nyr found himself within the Alvish lines with only Kha'el D'erth and Ghul Rwern at his side.

Seizing the opportunity, the Alvish soldiers shouted out as they set upon Nük T'nyr and his generals. For his part, Nük T'nyr grinned and waited, his sword thrust back and angled down—the ready position for fighting smallfolk. Kha'el D'erth and Ghul Rwern stood at Nük T'nyr's back in the same ready position.

The press of bodies closed in as the Alvish surged forward. When it seemed he must strike to stave off the charge, Nük T'nyr tossed his head back and laughed. He saw the clouds overhead breaking up and a yellow sun peeking through at midday. Closer and closer the ranks of his soldiers came.

Turning his attention back to the field and gate, he took the Alvish rush with the shield secured to his right forearm, an impenetrable barrier as he swept it through the Alvish ranks. Kha'el D'erth and Ghul Rwern did likewise. The three swept forward with their swords, cutting through the lines. Hundreds of Alvish bows thrummed together and the air filled with the humming of silver-winged shafts, forcing the three to use their shields as cover.

Arrows thudded against earth, flesh, and shield. Nük T'nyr emerged from the cover of his shield, sweeping the myriad of arrow shafts from his shield with his sword. He ignored the shafts sticking out of his flesh and instead surveyed the field. To his left, Ghul Rwern crouched behind his shield. To his right, Kha'el D'erth stood at the ready even as he clutched his shattered coat of mail and the bandages beneath with his free hand. Several small squads broke through the Alvish lines and joined them.

"Damned fools," Kha'el D'erth grunted, "They fight and fight and don't know they've already lost."

"Save for their shadowcrafting, they fight with honor," Nük T'nyr replied, offering Kha'el D'erth a pull of his flask. "Almost enough to earn my respect."

Kha'el D'erth took the liquid fire, emptied it, and grunted his thanks. "Cover!" He shouted as the Alvs in the front ranks dropped down to form a shield wall, and the archers behind them raised their bows.

The moments that followed stretched and slowed. Nük T'nyr looked out from the cover of his shield. He watched the Alvs. The Alvs watched him. Arrows found earth, flesh, and shield. Nük T'nyr recovered, swept the arrow shafts from his shield. He roared at the

Alvs as he charged. Kha'el D'erth and Ghul Rwern followed. Behind them were two squads, twelve and twenty strong each.

The work stayed close and bloody for what seemed many tolls. For every Alv he killed there were two or three waiting their turn. He never forgot his goal was the gate, and he worked toward it a stride at a time. The closer to the gate he came the stronger the Alvs seemed; and indeed the Alvs before him now, cloaked in black, stood head and shoulders taller than their brethren. They dual-wielded their swords with a skill he had not witnessed among their kind.

He studied their movements. Finding they worked in groups of two or three, he cast aside his shield and drew a second shorter blade to keep the Alvs from his kneecaps and hamstrings while he swept his great sword in wide-reaching arcs. To his right, an Alvish blade pierced Ghul Rwern's heart and he fell to his death. Nük T'nyr shouted, "Kurhri mo'rren, br'hm," to honor the other and mark his passing. A step behind, Kha'el D'erth echoed his words.

Nük T'nyr heard only the sound of his own breathing and the bloody work of his sword. He saw nothing but blood and steel. His arms began to ache, and still wave after wave of Alvish rushed in.

But then, in a great gale, the main host of his armies rejoined him. A mighty wall of shouting Empyrjurin, thousands strong, crushed into the Alvish ranks. A file of scarlet-clad Scarabaeid followed; and within this file walked the Praefect, his craft-clad arms raised and arcing white fire and blue lightning. Other Scarabaeid followed suit, raising their arms and arcing fire and lightning. For the first time in what seemed an age, Nük T'nyr looked up from death. He witnessed the sundering of the gates. The massive steel doors hung half on their hinges, twisted at impossible angels.

The battle swept past him then, with only Kha'el D'erth and

twenty-one others of the original sixty remaining. Far off in the direction of the distant highlands, warning horns sounded the arrival of reinforcements, surely from the other Alvish kingdoms, but they were too late. The city of S'amore burned.

—

Nük T'nyr was not there when the palace and inner keep fell. He left this glory to his soldiers, and glory in it they did even as they had to regroup on the plains to battle the Alvish reinforcements. That battle lasted through the afternoon and cost many, but by the time the yellow sun set the Empyrjurin ruled with few contenders to say otherwise.

Kha'el D'erth approached his king to give him the news. He had removed his chainmail and wrapped his wounds with fresh bandages. When he saw Nük T'nyr he knew he did not have to speak, but he did anyway. "The city is ours as night falls, true to your word."

Nük T'nyr carried a ceremonial blade and wore a gilded headdress. The blade in his hands seemed puny compared to the great blade now being oiled and tended by the master smith. "It is as the Praefect foretold and nothing more."

"Much more," Kha'el D'erth said, "I was there, I saw—the whole of your armies saw, Your Grace. You showed strength and resolve; you gave strength and resolve. G'rkyr T'nyr would have been proud."

The name of his dead father hardened Nük T'nyr's expression. Then he called out, saying "Kurhri mo'rren se hurren dar de'troden."

"Kurhri mo'rren," Kha'el D'erth replied after sinking down on one knee and bowing his head. When he raised his head he realized his error: He could not stand from this position. He could barely walk before and now he was stuck.

Nük T'nyr helped him to his feet, without comment. "You are my second now, Kha'el D'erth. See the Praefect. Have the Scarabaeid bind your wounds properly and renew you."

"I will," Kha'el D'erth replied. For a moment he wished to speak of Ghul Rwern, as he could see his king also wanted to speak of the other, but he pushed this down, and said, "The Praefect wants you there."

"And you will accompany me."

Kha'el D'erth nodded and walked with his king toward the city's nearby central square, where the Praefect and the Scarabaeid did their dark work on the Alvish survivors.

As he looked about the ruins of the city, Nük T'nyr said, "This world will be ours by cycle's end. Has he been named?"

"He has not. It is why the Praefect seeks you."

When they came to the square they found the Praefect and his crafters working a huddled mass of Alvs. Most Alvs bore what Kha'el D'erth thought were the royal colors of Dobehen, meaning they were of the royal guard and royal household, if not of the royal house of Dobehen itself.

A tiny Alvish woman with a wee babe in her arms caught his eye. She was one female whose face showed reserve rather than fear. Kha'el D'erth pointed her out to his king.

The Praefect put his boot across one Alv and commanded it to speak, his voice ringing with laughter. The Alv said nothing. The Praefect was about to press his boot and move on when the king approached. "You are in time for the questioning, Your Grace. I feared you would not—"

"Praefect L'kohn, you can obtain your amusement more readily elsewhere," Nük T'nyr said. It was a rebuke, and Kha'el D'erth nearly started at the hearing. "These are our enemies but honored enemies all the same."

"These have no honor, no shame. They are little more than beasts, and tiny squeamish little beasts at that."

"Beasts hiss and spit and run when they have the chance. Yet I saw none such. What I saw was worthy of my respect—and yours. You will give respect."

Kha'el D'erth hid a glow of pride from his face. G'rkyr T'nyr had never dared to openly confront the Scarabaeid, and here was his son on the eve of his first victory—putting not only the Scarabaeid, but also their Praefect, in place. He made a mental note to increase vigilance among his watchers upon his return to Jurin. The Praefect would not do anything openly and indeed acceded, but would have to be watched in case he decided to seek retribution later.

"They refuse to cooperate. They will not point out their royals."

"And you ask your questions with your boots?"

The Praefect glared but did not reply. The look was to remind Nük T'nyr who held the leash of his power.

Kha'el D'erth stepped between the king and the master crafter. "Your victory will be the talk of Jurin, Your Grace. Our people will know you led our victory and that the Scarabaeid brought down the gates of S'amore. What's more, the Alvish have proven worthy adversaries. Long has it been since I've had such a good fight."

Nük T'nyr clasped Kha'el's shoulder in a show of respect. "My father was wrong to keep you as his third. You deserved to be his second."

"I am your second," Kha'el said. "That is what he knew I would be."

Nük T'nyr looked to the Praefect. "Indeed," he said. He turned his attention to the Alvs who filled the square. "Who among you speaks for you?" he asked in the language of the Alvish.

Kha'el D'erth stepped forward when no one spoke and pointed to the Alvish woman with the baby. Nük T'nyr gave sign of agreement.

Kha'el D'erth plucked them from the crowd, holding the woman with her baby in the palm of his hand. "Who among you speaks for you?" he repeated.

"I will speak," the Alvish woman said. "I am Queen Athania of Dobehen."

"Speak truth," Kha'el D'erth said impatiently in the language of the Jurin people. "My king has shown great restraint and given great respect."

"I speak truth," Queen Athania replied in the Jurin language, her gaze and voice steady even as she edged the child back.

"Your king," Kha'el D'erth said impatiently. "Where is he?"

"Do you seek the king of kings or my king?" the queen asked.

Kha'el D'erth felt closed in as Nük T'nyr and the Praefect pressed forward. "We seek your husband, King of Dobehen."

"You seek one who will not be found."

Nük T'nyr studied the Alvish queen, seeing a calm akin to one he found in battle. "Kurhri mo'rren," he told her.

"To blessed death," the queen replied.

"A slow death for him," Kha'el heard the Praefect say in a low voice. "Very slow and very painful."

And for Kha'el, that was the end of it. The Praefect took the queen and her child away, and he never saw either again.

His king turned to regard him and then the battle-weary soldiers who encircled the square and waited in long files running down the streets.

"Today we have the first victory on our road to rising again," the king said. "Today is the Day of the Reckoning. Our Day of the Atonement, though distant, will come. On that day we will know freedom as a people."

Battle weary and wounded, the soldiers still raised their voices and their swords, their shouts reaching out to the highlands many leagues distant and their boots shaking the earth.

PART I
KARTHOLD

The Cycle 11226
Drakón Standard

The ageless rose up, tall as mountains
And breathed fire across the hundred worlds.
—Translated from the *Secti Monter Drakón,*
or *Book of the Dragons*

CHAPTER ONE

All across the dark, windswept lands, a million slaves from a hundred broken worlds and their slavered beasts toiled in and about the pits created by their excavations, unearthing and reclaiming relics of a forgotten age for the never-seen gods of their age. The overlords kept watch from high above, looking down on the labor. Now and again, as the tocks and tolls passed, a cry of discovery would issue forth. Then those closest to the caller would rush in by the hundreds and thousands, toiling as one until the new artifact was unearthed and dragged away by ropes and mute beasts.

Sometimes, after an unearthing, an overlord would grant reward to all laborers in the sector, allowing them to pause in their work and partake of liquid bread spread freely at the overlord's beckoning, offered as if a gift. Rastín was one of the few who never took the offered drink, relying instead on a pouch of water and hard black biscuits he secreted away and packed each morning before the day's labors began.

After an unearthing an overlord would always grant reward to the laborer who made the discovery, descending from the heavens on his platform until he was eight or nine spans from the ground, stepping down living stairs and across a living carpet formed by the workers until he stood before the recipient of his gift. He would then raise his staff of office to the heavens while calling out to the ageless gods, and then he would touch the tip of his staff to the top of the recipient's head. In the end, the recipient would thank and bless the overlord even as lightning flashed from the heavens and ripped him from the fields and this life.

Such an end was said to be a blessing, and every worker in every corner of the dark land was expected to pay tribute to it by crying out to the heavens and begging for such glory for themselves. Even the dimwitted beasts would join in, though they had no tongues and could only make guttural croonings. Rastín did not believe such an end brought glory, however, finding only the futility and folly of it. So while others cried with their blessings to the ageless, he exclaimed muddled curses, secretly damning the ageless with every foul word of every foul language he had learned in his short life.

By evenfall this day, Rastín had cursed the ageless an unprecedented seventeen times, and there was palpable tension in the air as he joined the lines before the thousand-fold gates to return to the realm of the overlords. A daring few whispered of the day's many unearthings and the expectations of a major discovery—possibly that of a cornerstone—soon. Such a find would make the discoverer one of the exalted, raising him or her from drudgery and postponing the blessed parting until such time as the ageless themselves willed the exalted from this life.

Rastín had no desire to become an exalted, yet he could not help thinking about what such a future would mean for him and the companion he chose. It was the one true dream left to one who otherwise had no aspirations, no dreams, no escape save blessed death.

Because his dig site was far from the thousand-fold gates, there were many ahead of him by the time he joined the lines. In the distance he could hear the night criers as the darkening skies and the disembarking masses emboldened the criers to emerge from their shrouded hiding places.

The overlords hovered high above on their floating platforms, gathered in clusters. Their staffs of office, transformed into fiery whips with long sinewy tendrils, lashed out occasionally at the empty spaces between the illuminated lines and the deepening shadows. Rastín knew this without having to look back as he began to make his way forward through the lines. His youth and lineage ensured that he had only to touch a hand to the shoulder of anyone blocking his way to be allowed to pass, so in this way he made his way toward the front of his line.

Reaching the gate platform, he stepped forward and made ready for the brief passage between this land and that of the overlords. A dense bunch of mute beasts moved before the gate, however, refusing to pass through or allow others to do so. Two guardians, one on either side of the gate, brought their weighted chains around and carved a swath through the gathered beasts. Yet this did not stop them from blocking Rastín's passage until several other laborers moved ahead of him and went through the gate.

Shaken by the incident but resolved to leave the dark land, Rastín stepped into the gate. Bone-chilling cold found him for an instant, and then just as suddenly he was walking through one of the colossal passageways that led through the massive fortifications surrounding the immortal city of the ageless.

The cool, moist air in the corridor was invigorating after his long day. As he emerged from the corridor, open skies and mammoth towers greeted him. The way paths between the towers were crowded, the air paths no better as peoples and beasts of all manner abided in the city. He was excited about the prospect of speaking with his father and conferring with him about the possibility of yet another cornerstone find, and for this reason he made his way rapidly to the encampment of the people of Élvemere, his people.

His family's pavilion was in the farthest corner of the camp, its aging silk and cloth a reminder of a past lost to the mists of time. Looking at the tattered silk and cloth fluttering in the wind, he could not help mourning a time he had never known, for his father's mind lived in this time.

Alborn and Djerg, who stood guard outside the pavilion, stepped aside as he approached. He returned their gesture of respect with a kind word of greeting. "Pritish," he told them in the language of ceremony. It was a greeting of praise and honor and the guards returned it heartily, for in this place none were slaves or masters.

King Enáthon Túrring was lying in his once-garish bed of ruined silks and satins with many bloated pillows to keep him upright. Rastín no longer noticed the ruin of his father's body or the serpent magi who kept his father alive, even though little flesh remained under the blankets.

He knew the ageless maintained his father because his father kept order, and without his father there would be chaos. He did not resent the serpent magi, but he knew their duties included keeping watch and reporting back to their masters.

"Salus, salut," he told his father, again using the language of ceremony. It was tradition, speaking to his father's health and honor. After kissing the living side of his father's face he knelt and bowed his head, waiting for his father to speak.

"Dny, my son," the old king said, the living side of his face suddenly showing color. "Sadly, you have only just missed your mother."

Still kneeling, Rastín Dnyarr Túrring looked up at his father. He said nothing of the fact that his mother had gone to the blessed land many cycles ago. Instead, he smiled and said, "I should have liked to have seen her. She would have been pleased at my discoveries this day."

"She would have been," his father said turning his good eye to regard his son, his dead eye continuing to stare off into the distance. Then he muttered something about food and drink.

Rastín knew the food and drink was for him, because his father rarely ate now. He stood, poured a glass of water from a silver pitcher. He drank deeply, and then ate the leftovers from his father's discarded meal. The food quenched a hunger in him that he had not noticed until he started eating.

While he ate, his father spoke of the flat, open grassland beyond his pavilion and the forest that was just beyond the line of sight. Though this place existed for them only in dream now, Rastín knew it well, for it was the land of his people and his father spoke of it often. "Your mother walks to the trees. She wants to speak to the ancient ones. Will you meet her before she returns?"

"I will, father. I will take your stallion, Windrunner. I should like to speak with the ancient ones myself."

"Good, good. She will be so pleased to see you, and the two of you can talk. You know my time comes, I can sense it, and so it will be you who must lead our people. Do you honor the old ways? Do you sing the praises of your kin?"

"I do, father. I honor always those in the blessed lands. I pray for them to protect and keep me on the path."

"This is good, my son. You will make a fine high king. The kings of all lands will swear fealty to you, and our people will regain our rightful place."

"On my honor, as I live and breathe, father, I will restore our family name." As he said this, Rastín hid a tear that came to his eye, for the truth of those words was too close to his heart. And although this great sadness was fleeting, it was enough to interrupt his second consciousness—the self he kept hidden to all save his father's second self.

His fingers lost their grip on his father's arm. The lost grip broke the connection. His father uttered a stray word—a single word, no more, no less, but it was an unexpected word for those who kept watch and thought they saw and heard all.

Rastín pretended not to hear the word. Instead, he picked up the silver pitcher and filled a cup, then helped his father drink from the cup, careful not to raise the cup too quickly as his father could only drink from one side of his mouth. He dabbed the side of his father's face with a cloth, and then returned to the affectedly proper speech to which the magi were accustomed. "Father, I should be going soon. Do you have a message to pass along to mother?"

"I should like to go with you, my son," his father replied, "but as I cannot—"

Rastín's second self heard no more of the other self's conversation as he continued with his account of the dig. "Seventeen unearthings is unprecedented. The whisperers say a cornerstone is at hand."

"Indeed," his father said, "the final one at last then."

"The last, are you sure?"

"We are elf kind, High King of Élvemere. We see it, fully formed."

Rastín had not meant to offend his father. "What will come of it?"

"It will open the path to a place not seen since the Firstborn walked and dreamed. A place both outside time and within it. In this place, you could live a lifetime, return to our place, and find that millennia have passed or that no time has passed at all. From this place, the ageless will rule over all living things for all time. I can see this as clearly as I've ever seen—"

Rastín interrupted, speaking quickly while the vision was at its strongest, "What will become of us? What will become of our people?"

"The ageless," Túrring began to say, but further words became impossible as he gurgled and gasped for breath as blood bubbled up from his lungs.

Rastín collapsed his thoughts and became one within himself. He picked up the churn bucket from the floor and put it under his father's chin while leaning his father forward with his other hand. While his father coughed and sputtered, he said a silent prayer to his mother. "Protect and keep us," he whispered, imagining her waiting for them both in the blessed land.

CHAPTER TWO

Outside his father's pavilion, Rastín, son of the High King of Élvemere, received no extra comforts. He was treated with deference, but beyond this he was regarded no differently than any other of his kind. In the dark before dawn, he awoke with everyone else when the first toll sounded. He ate, readied himself for the long day, and went with the others when the second toll sounded.

In the predawn twilight, the immortal city of the ageless was at its worst. Not only were the way paths and air paths overflowing with all manner of peoples and beasts, but also the great towers were alive—breathing fire, venting smoke and ash. At times, the ground beneath his feet rumbled and quaked as the towers rumbled and quaked. This brought with it the sounds of the damned, which surged forth over and over in howls and wailing.

Rastín despised the ageless because of those sounds. Backbreaking labor was one thing, torture and damnation another. To him, the ageless were lower than the dumb beasts who worked the excavations.

Suddenly, a stinging chain ripped apart the flesh of his shoulder, arousing him to conscious thoughts. He stared blankly at the gate guardian and quickly moved through the gate. Bitter cold and darkness followed.

For an instant, in this place between the ancient city and the windswept plains of a distant land, Rastín found solace. In this darkness, no one or no thing could touch him. He was beyond everything and everyone. Here he lived for two heartbeats a day, reconciled his two selves, and became one with both for those instants. And in those instants, he knew all that both had seen and heard. The sting of leaving this place behind was no less than the sting of the chain, and it left emptiness within that nothing else filled.

As he emerged from the thousand-fold gates into the dark land, he saw, a league or more distant, jagged mountains of purple stone. He marched with the others of his kind a hundred abreast toward these mountains and the dig site where he would spend the day laboring under blood-red skies—the same strange skies that had darkened the skin of his once fair people until it was a deep, lustrous silver.

He arrived at the dig site, sweating but not tired. The forced march was oddly cleansing and renewing. In a way, it prepared him for the day's labor. With pick and ax, he began to break the hard surface and dig. Mute beasts carried away rock and soil with ropes and carts. All the while, the overlords looked on from their floating platforms.

Early in the day, he knew he was close to a find. This frightened him because he did not want to become one of the blessed. He did his best to work other areas of his excavation pit, but he could only delay for so long. By midday, he had dug down an additional five spans—more than half his height—in all areas of the pit save one. He was about to begin digging in this area when a cry of discovery came forth from the far side of the excavation site.

Relieved, he heaved his pick and ax to his shoulder and raced with the others toward the caller, then worked with the others as one until a massive metallic shard was unearthed. Because this was the first discovery of the day, the regional overlord was both pleased and displeased as he stepped from his platform down the living stairs formed by the workers.

Rastín and another formed the bottom step of the living stair, and it was here the overlord stood as he surveyed the find. Rastín dared not make a sound as he strained under the weight. He dared not look up, but he could not help the feeling of awe that swept through him.

This was the closest he had ever been to one of the exalted. He seemed to be but a step away from the ageless gods that had subjugated his people. He could not hold back the flood of hatred that raced through him and yet felt humbled, powerless in the exalted's presence.

As the overlord stepped across a living carpet of Rastín's people, Rastín breathed a sigh of relief. He turned his head to watch the overlord until the other stood before the worker who had made the find. Rastín was surprised to recognize Holsteb. He remembered that Holsteb had once been kindly toward him, so it angered him even more when the good man was forced to his knees to accept an unwelcome reward.

Unwanted or not, the overlord touched the tip of his staff to Holsteb's head and imparted the gift of the ageless. At the end, in the last moments as his flesh was torn and rent, Holsteb thanked and blessed the overlord and the ageless. Then lightning flashed from the heavens, and Holsteb was no more.

Every worker and every beast in every corner of the dark land paid tribute to the blessing by crying out. Rastín wanted more than anything to stand and scream a curse against the ageless and damn them, but the overlord was close and getting closer as he walked back across the living carpet toward the platform. So instead, he cried out with a tribute, telling himself his tribute was to Holsteb and not to the blessed event.

Rastín was still crying out when he felt the overlord's foot on his back. For a moment he shouldered the overlord's full weight, nearly buckling; but he ground his teeth, closed his eyes, and fought to remain steady. Instead of climbing, however, the overlord pivoted, turning to face the mass of workers as he granted reward and the liquid bread flowed freely. Under the strain, Rastín blacked out, but knew he must have succeeded in holding his own when the overlord's platform began rising into the sky and he no longer felt as if his back would burst.

Shouldering his pick and ax, he trudged off to find a new area in which to dig. Although there were many diggers, there were scores of open areas; he chose one of these. It took the rest of the day to excavate a pit ten spans deep and twenty spans across.

By evenfall, Rastín was spent. He made his way very slowly to the thousand-fold gates. His position among the old and infirm must have seemed an invitation to the night criers, for they howled in the shadows not far off. A part of him would have welcomed the end they would bring. Death in this way would cheat the ageless, because it would bring no glory to them or anyone else.

The fiery tendrils of an overlord's whip lapping at the darkness just behind him stirred Rastín into a run. He pulled the old one to his right along with him, urging others to run as well. For a moment, as he turned his head back, he could see many pairs of glowing red eyes staring at him from the darkness.

Reaching the gate platform, he pushed the others ahead of him. Because the old one could barely put one foot in front of the other, Rastín led him to the gate. The two guardians, who stood one to either side of the gate, brought their weighted chains around as if to strike him for trying to enter the gate two abreast, but apparently thought better of it and stopped midstrike.

As Rastín stepped into the gate's magical field and the bone-chilling cold, he glimpsed his father's face—not the ruined face of the present, but the noble face from a past Rastín had never known. Emerging into the colossal passageway that led through the fortifications into the city, his thoughts turned inward. This day the dearth of discoveries was as remarkable as the abundance the previous day.

He was slow to realize, as he made his way to the central laborers' encampment, that none of his kind were in the corridor with him. Instead, he was in a corridor filled with the mute beasts who carried and pulled things and did the other heavy work in the excavations. Before this day he had not realized his kind and their kind were separated in some way on the return, but now it was not only readily apparent, it was unpleasant and unnerving.

Entering the vast city with its great stone edifices, he did not find the familiar path to the central camp. Instead, he stood before an endless span of twisted serpentine towers; directly in front of him was a sloping passageway with arches on both sides that looked like it would take him under the towers.

Faced with the unknown and a break from his routine, he felt suddenly afraid and alone. He tried to go back into the corridor and return to the gate platform, but the moving mass of beasts prevented this. Soon he found he was being ushered forward toward the passageway beneath the towers.

Although confused, he did not allow panic to set in. Cycles earlier when he was taken to his first dig, in what was already without question the most terrifying experience of his young life, he had been slow to the gates and had come face to face with a pack of night criers. The fact that he survived the encounter led many to believe the ageless smiled upon him and that he walked within their grace. But it was his father's council on the previous day that had saved him.

Túrring had told him, "No matter what you encounter in the dark land, you must find calm and resolve not to show anguish, sorrow, or fear. If you show any of these weak emotions, our enemies, even those amongst our own people, will use those weaknesses against you and you will live forever after in fear."

"I will make you proud, father," Rastín promised. "I will not show weakness."

His father finished, saying, "You will be allowed to cry later beyond the hearing of others if need be."

And indeed he had cried later, sobbing long into the night though he was weary to his bones from the day's labors.

So now, as then, he closed his eyes and waited. Seeking to find inner calm, he breathed in deeply and exhaled slowly. He opened his eyes only after a ten count of heartbeats, finding clarity and strength instead of confusion and fear.

He stepped forward unafraid and started through the passageway, because it seemed the only way to go; but one of the she-beasts in the moving mass stepped around him and blocked his way. Although she could not speak, her eyes told him that she meant him no harm. For his part, his eyes told her that he had no ill intensions toward her, and his lack of fear seemed to calm her.

The calm was fleeting. Suddenly she was upon him, grabbing him and dragging him into a dark recess where a large drainage pipe emptied sewage from the towers above into a narrow maw. He started to speak, to question her as he would have one of his kind, but stopped when she looked puzzled. When he started to speak again, she rushed a mud-covered hand to his mouth. The hand, though clawed and thick with fur, had five digits. One of these was like a thumb in that it was shorter and thicker than the other digits and adapted for grasping, yet it did not seem as dexterous as his own thumb.

Forcibly, she stripped him of his thick shirt and began covering him with the sewage-laden mud. He tried to resist, but the she-beast was surprisingly strong. Later he emerged from the dark recess only when she allowed him to. Covered in mud and muck from head to heel, he appeared as any other mud-covered creature, moving through the passageway.

Gripping his elbow, the she-beast began to lead him. Rastín did not resist, but he did move cautiously. The passageway opened into a vast courtyard surrounded on all sides by the serpentine towers. The she-beast led him deeper into the yard. Grass-covered hillocks dotted with trees gave the perception that he was in endless grassland—the kind of grassy land of which his father spoke; but as one born a slave in this land he had never seen.

Carved into the hillocks were holes; and within the holes he saw movement, shadows deeper and darker than the rich, brown earth. Despite himself, he began to tremble. And as he did, the she-beast's demeanor hardened, as did her viselike grip on his arm. She began to pull him around like a possession, a thing, a toy. Her toy.

She abruptly pulled him into one of the holes. At once they came to an antechamber with crude furnishings of a sort he had never seen before. The interior of the hole was dimly lit by something similar to a torch, but it gave off neither heat nor smoke.

Beyond the large, central round of the antechamber was a room with a dark hole in the middle surrounded by rough stones. The she-beast lifted him off the ground, moving him much like one of the dilapidated beams at the dig site, and put him in this hole.

To his surprise, he found the hole was filled with water, waist deep and cool. The first time the she-beast dunked him under the water he thought she was trying to drown him, and his struggles brought her into the water with him. Once she was in the water with him, she began dunking and swishing him as if he were her life-sized doll.

Beneath her tangled mass of hair, he saw her eyes glowing in the pale light. Locks of her hair, thick like a serpent's body, were twisted and tied. As she moved, her hair moved, shifting as if a hundred tendrils of a many-headed snake. The dark land had such snakes, and he now thought that the she-beast was a snake person not unlike those his father talked about. These people were from a time in his father's childhood when his father and his grandfather journeyed freely between the realms.

The very idea of walking free carried Rastín's thoughts away. He stopped resisting, allowing a bit of himself to slip away with each breath until it was as if he was no longer present—almost as if what was happening to him now was a dream from another's life. The dreamer was cleansed, rinsed, and bedded by the she-beast. The living, thinking, breathing Rastín walked free with his father and grandfather across flat, open grassland he had never seen with his own eyes but knew well. It was the land of his people, his land by right of birth.

CHAPTER THREE

Rastín woke to the movements of the she-beast. She covered him with mud, applying thick layers to his entire body. Not understanding what was happening or why, he resisted; but his strength was no match for hers.

Finally, sullen and beaten into submission, he gave in. Later, he ate and drank what she offered. He followed her when the time came to go to the dark land. Caked in mud and clad only in a wrapped cloth, he looked more like a he-beast than one of his own kind.

In one of the many wide corridors leading from the immortal city of the ageless, he joined the moving mass of beasts, quickly finding himself in the dark land on the other side of the gate. When he tried to rejoin his kind and moved to pick up tools for the dig, the she-beast tackled him and dragged him away to the ropes and carts. Soon afterward, a gargantuan he-beast was placing a harness around his neck. The harness, made of wood and leather, extended down his chest to his waist. It formed an exterior cage over his small frame and had hooks of several different types to which he could attach ropes and tools.

Before he comprehended what was happening, the large he-beast attached ropes to the harness; Rastín found himself pulling one of the large, eight-wheeled cart trains piled high with ropes, pulleys, and excavation gear. Although he had worked for many cycles in the excavations and was as strong as any full-grown male of his kind, he faltered under the load and managed only a few steps. The she-beast was there in an instant, pushing the cart train as he pulled, and then pulling with a second harness as they climbed into the high lands.

Although he had labored among them, the world of the beasts was entirely unknown to him. Early in the day, he was overcome with an inexplicable fear that the overlords hovering overhead would see him for who he was. This fear intensified whenever the she-beast was near him. It kept him focused on something other than the backbreaking work. It also alerted him whenever the enforcers with their whips walked near.

As a laborer among his own kind, he had been watchful of the overlords but not of the enforcers. As long as he did his work, he need not fear the enforcers' whips. He feared their whips now, though, and he wore that fear despite his best efforts to the contrary.

To calm himself, he whispered a prayer to his mother. "Protect and keep me," he implored.

He learned quickly that any time he thought he was alone, he was not. The she-beast was always near even if he could not see her. From time to time she took dirt from the earth, mixed it with water from a leather bag at her waist, and then applied this mixture to any exposed area of his flesh. As the day wore on, he realized the thick cake of mud kept away the sting of the ropes and harness. It also was useful to close open wounds, and already he had four long gashes on his exposed torso: two from an enforcer's whip for failing to keep pace, one from a cart slip, and one from the she-beast herself for attempting to speak to one of his kind.

By midday Rastín could barely stand. His spirit was broken. Broken by the whip. Broken by the work. Broken by his inexplicable fear. Staggering, he dreamed he walked off the cart trail and that the cart train he was pulling followed him down the side of the excavation pit, rolling over him and then dragging him down with it. He felt every impact as his body was tossed about. He heard the tumultuous roar of the cart train as it careened downward, felt the tremors when the first cart exploded into splinters as it slammed into the bottom of the pit. The second cart followed, breaking apart in similar fashion.

When he hit the ground, he felt as if the world had stopped. His first thought was that the harness cage was shattered and he was free. His second thought was that he felt no agony or perhaps that his body was so racked with pain that it had overwhelmed his senses. He saw the face of his father whispering words that he could not understand. Finally, he thought about death. He felt sure death had found him, but he was not afraid. In an odd way, thoughts of death were calming, bringing him back to the here and now.

As he came around, he realized it was well past midday. The she-beast was tending to him, giving him food and water. He knew then that it was the time of the second meal. Across from him, less than a chain away, he could see those of his kind taking their meal breaks.

He thought of ways he could signal them to come to his aid. Subtly he tried to make them aware of his presence. They took no notice of him, however. This angered him until he realized that before the previous day he could not honestly say that he had ever noticed any of the beast kind. They were the faceless, the unseen, and the unknown.

Only a preternatural sense of caution kept further action in check. Somehow, he knew must not continue to try to draw the attention of his kind, so he resolved to wait until he knew more about what was happening to him and why. Although he tried his best to hide this change within himself, the she-beast noticed the subtle shift in his demeanor. She seemed to approve of it, and to show this she moved closer.

By evenfall, only the she-beast kept Rastín on his feet, and she did so with surprising care. As packs of beasts moved to the thousand-fold gates, she helped him to the gates without drawing the attention of the overlords and enforcers. She moved with him across the platform and into the gate. It was the first time Rastín had ever entered the way gate with another. What happened in that brief moment he would not be able to understand until much later, but it was perhaps the reason the gate guardians ensured his people entered the gates one at a time.

Everything after entering the gate was a blur. Rastín barely managed to maintain consciousness. He vaguely remembered the she-beast bathing him and that he slept close against her mane to keep warm. When he awoke in the morning, it was as if his senses were on fire. He heard a tiny buzzer flying in the far corner of the room. When he looked for it, not only could he see it, but it was as if the buzzer were right before him. He could smell his blood on the buzzer and knew it had been feeding on him. In the blood, he could smell iron and earth and so much more.

He tried to stand, but as he did so the room seemed to shift under his feet. The she-beast was at his side in an instant, guiding him, acting as his legs and arms. Looking at her as she held him steady, he was suddenly aware of minute movements—gestures involving the muscles of the face, the eyes, and the ears—that conveyed meaning and became to his mind words. She was telling him something but he did not understand, and this frustrated her.

She repeated herself several times and finally he understood. She was telling him her name. Her name was Akharran. She was of the Wërg people. He tried to tell her he was Rastín Dnyarr Túrring of the Élvemere people. But she became frustrated and cut him off—such a long name made no sense to her. Finally, he told her that he was Dny. This seemed to please her as she responded in gestures that said, "Yes, Dny."

As she repeated this, Rastín saw such movements for what they were for the first time. They were language. The beasts were neither mute nor dumb. They simply communicated in a way no one else understood.

At his understanding, the she-beast did something that he did not understand at the time but would later know as emotion expressed through movement. These were her tears, but they represented overwhelming joy, not sadness. Gesturing in her language, Rastín tried to ask what she had done to him, but her response was unexpected.

"Hurry, danger," she told him.

"Yes, hurry, danger," Rastín replied using gestures.

Rastín followed her as she left the hole and made her way back to the transition corridors. She did not speak to him as they walked or as they worked out in the dark land. Although Rastín found this odd, he did not try to speak to her, either.

Several days passed before he was comfortable enough with her language to try to reach beyond the basics of things like food, shelter, and work. Akharran seemed pleased with this progression but avoided the deeper, more meaningful discussions for which Rastín longed.

While walking and working among other Wërg, Rastín began to

learn things Akharran may not have wanted him to know. For instance, the Wërg constantly passed messages among themselves using their expressive language. Messages passed in this way up and down corridors, across the Wërg camp, and throughout the fields in the dark land.

The Wërg were more intelligent than Rastín had ever imagined. Their language was terse but not without its nuances, but he was convinced the Wërg would not understand poetry, books, or music. Such things would have taken too long to convey and would have seemed wasteful—lavish.

Yet he learned the Wërg language also could be conveyed using rhythmic touch. The first time he tried rhythmic touching with Akharran, she became angry and made gestures that were the equivalent of shouting. She did not speak to him all that day, but by evenfall her mood seemed to shift and she seemed to forgive him. Later, Rastín asked, "What wrong done?"

Akharran pretended not to understand, which made Rastín angry. He ignored her until she snuggled closer to him and told him, "Great wrong done." Using only her touch she told him, "Father, mother. Sister, brother. Son, daughter."

Together, Rastín knew this conveyed the sense of family. He asked her, "Only father, mother, sister, brother, son, daughter?"

She replied with what he understood as "clan."

He rolled over and ignored her after that, falling asleep until morning. When he awoke, he convinced himself that if there was fault to be assigned, the fault was his, because Akharran must have known what he felt. Deep down he saw Akharran as a person but saw the rest of the Wërg people as beasts—talking beasts, but beasts just the same. After that, he forced himself to think of the Wërg as kithfolk rather than beasts. He told himself that she was Akharran of the Wërg people, and the Wërg were a good people who meant no harm. As he thought this, he absentmindedly expressed it by touch as well, which caused a commotion among the Wërg who walked with him in the transition corridor. Akharran calmed the tumult quickly, but in so doing betrayed something she clearly had not meant for Rastín to know. Akharran told the Wërg around her that she was Wërg and was not to be doubted. It was the equivalent of his father saying, "We are elf kind, High King of Élvemere." He knew in an instant what it meant; it meant Akharran was not just any Wërg. She was a queen or as close to such as her kind had.

For the past few days they had entered the gate together, sharing themselves with each other in those moments in ways that Rastín did not quite understand but had began to look forward to. Today, however, Akharran pushed Rastín ahead of her, forcing him into the gate alone.

Entering the dark land alone, he felt the sudden sting of loss—loss of a thing he could not quite name. For a few heartbeats he seemed juxtaposed in time and place, as if living two lives. In one, he was not just with the Wërg but a Wërg. In the other, he was elf kind and knew his father waited for him to return from the day's labors.

Akharran set him to rights, wrenching him from the gate platform and out into the dark land. She was increasingly on edge whenever they worked the excavation site. It did not help matters that the last unearthing had been Holsteb's, days ago, and with each passing day the overlords and the enforcers became increasingly brutal and merciless.

The tackmaster Zrteth placed a harness of wood and leather around his neck and waist, and then attached ropes to the harness. He said nothing to Rastín, but he had plenty to say to Akharran before sending both on their way with a large eight-wheeled cart train overflowing with ropes, pulleys, and excavation gear.

Together they moved out across the fields and up into the high lands. Rastín did most of the work, as Akharran seemed to want nothing to do with pulling and pushing the cart. At the dig site, Akharran became so distant that Rastín dared to speak to her openly, asking her, "Still wrong?"

Akharran's response was to throw the boulder she was shouldering at him instead of into the cart. Rastín's quick reflexes allowed him to jump easily out of the boulder's path. Looking up as he did so, he saw Akharran express emotion in the way of his people—feelings of sorrow and anguish that reflected Rastín's own conflicted feelings.

At midday, Akharran spoke to him openly for the first time, telling him, "Madness comes. Danger, great danger."

Rastín sat beside her. "Madness?"

"Angry madness. Danger."

Rastín tried to understand what she was telling him. When she repeated herself and he smelled her fear, he finally understood. He replied with the exact same phrasing, "Angry madness. Danger." Then he dared to speak a word aloud in his own language. That word was "war."

Akharran erupted into a frenzy, capturing his expression just as he said it—a mixture of sorrow and anguish—and passed this out to other Wërg. It became their watchword. Akharran and other Wërg repeated it over and over in the transition corridor on the return from the dark land, and Rastín felt self-loathing build within him each time they did so. He was the one to give a name to the thing the Wërg had never known before the ageless came to their world.

In her hollow, Akharran did something she had never done before. Instead of sending Rastín to the bathing hole, she sat him down and commanded him to speak to her. Rastín defied her and went to the bathing hole instead. He lingered in the cool waters longer than usual; and although he wanted to refuse food, his hunger was such that he could not.

Akharran looked pleased when he joined her in the large round and approached the eating stone. She insisted he sit beside her and he did so. On the eating stone, she had arranged more food and drink than he had ever seen before. Wërg food consisted mostly of roots and tubers, much of which was grown in dark chambers within the hollows where they lived. Some roots and tubers were served raw. Others were cooked, dried, or pounded into powder or paste. Some powders and pastes were mixed with water to make flavored drinks of a sort he had never had before.

Akharran's close attention to him as he ate told him she wanted something from him but either did not know how to ask or was waiting for the right time to ask. He was surprised when she said nothing and instead made it clear she wanted something else entirely. Rastín complied, giving himself to Akharran as she gave herself to him.

CHAPTER FOUR

Days among the Wërg turned into many turnings, and Rastín began to yearn for a return to his people. He wanted more than anything to see his father and speak aloud in his own tongue. Akharran saw this and understood his longing. In the dark land while they worked, she would extend certain kindnesses to him that she extended to no other Wërg. These kindnesses helped him endure the heightened cruelty of the overlords and enforcers as they claimed of flesh what they could not claim through discovery. Discoveries in the dark land had become things of the past, and everyone suffered as a result.

Rastín was glad the Wërg were a hardy people who found ways to sustain themselves. Other peoples were less fortunate. Day by day there were fewer and fewer working the excavations. Whole peoples faded away, and Rastín saw their kind no more.

This day as they returned from the highlands, Akharran was distant, and Rastín did not understand why. It was not until they were within sight of the thousand-fold gates that she grabbed his arm, signaling him to stop. When he turned to face her, she pulled his hand to her stomach and then said, "War." If she were elf kind, he would have sworn that she had tears in her eyes when she said it. He had never seen Akharran or any Wërg express emotion in this way, so he cast the thought aside.

He tried to speak, but she interrupted him. "Danger, great danger," she told him. "Rastín Dnyarr Túrring of the Élvemere people must now remember."

After she said it, she moved toward the gates with a speed Rastín had never seen before. He could not keep up with her, and he soon lost sight of her among the masses waiting to return to the immortal city of the ageless. He wandered through the lines, searching for her, risking the chains, ignoring the whips from high above that sought to keep him in his place.

It was Wërg who herded him toward the platform, often taking blows in his stead, and Wërg who saw him through the gate though he entered the gate alone. The bitter cold of the space between brought a feeling of such loneliness that it seemed his soul shook with the ache of it. Indeed, he emerged from the gate shaking. Walking through the transition corridor and into the city, he hardly saw anything.

Only when he was standing before the ashes of his father's pavilion did he realize that he was back among his kind. But as he stood there, caked in mud, looking like a thing he was not, he might as well have been invisible. His people did not see him.

There was one other among the ashes of his father's pavilion. His name was Alborn, and he was a trusted guard. Rastín had not seen the old guard at first because he was kneeling in prayer.

Rastín quietly approached Alborn. The aged guard did not turn or start at the sound of Rastín's approach. Instead he waited until Rastín was standing directly behind him, and then said quietly, "You have returned. I hear you in your gait. Under earth, leather, and wood, I smell you; but I do not see you."

As Alborn stood and turned, Rastín understood there was much unsaid behind those words, for the Alborn he saw was not the Alborn he had known. The Alborn he had known carried a great sword. He had kind eyes and a face that spoke quietly of respect held close. The Alborn standing before him carried a walking stick, had no eyes and a face with cheeks so hollow that they seemed to be those of the dead. Rastín wondered if Alborn had passed on and only lingered here before setting off for the blessed land.

That illusion was broken when Alborn gripped Rastín's arm to steady himself and said, "Quickly now, we must be away."

Alborn led him to a tent on the far side of the burned area where King Túrring's pavilion had stood. Once inside the tent, Alborn closed and secured the entrance.

"Your father joined your mother in the blessed land four turnings back to the day, to the toll," Alborn urgently explained. "At the end I thought there was only one thing he longed for in this life, and that was to see your return. It was a mistake on my part, the first of many.

"In the instant of your father's passing, the serpent magi departed, never to be seen again. Chaos found us as soon as it was discovered you had not returned. I did my best to keep this quiet. I pretended for days that you were among us, grieving your father. My eyes, my cost. Gouged out by one of the ageless themselves.

"Your father's rivals set fire to the pavilion. A loyal few could not prevent it, nor stop the flames from spreading."

Rastín wrapped his arms around the old guard and wept openly. "You did your duty as best as you could, better than anyone else could have done. You've paid such a price for loyalty, and I have nothing to repay you with."

"My loyalty cannot be bought or sold, paid or unpaid. My family has served since the reckoning—the day the Élvemere people were enslaved—and before. Though you have not been crowned, you are my king now as your father was before."

"Shodjen—"

"—and others. The factions are many, numbering more than ever imagined. Nearly every great house. Nearly every great family. We are a fractured people now. If you were to return into this chaos, you would suffer Djerg's fate or worse."

"Dear, loyal, faithful Djerg, too?"

"His body hangs where it happened. I dare not fetch it down, though I did not hesitate to cut his heart through when they started on him. My vows, my cost; my life spared for renouncing you. Djerg begged me to do what I must. I did what must be done because there was no other to do it, yet at the cost of my soul."

Suddenly feeling older than his cycles, Rastín spoke with his father's voice and his father's words. "There is no shame, Alborn son of Jfe, for doing what must be done."

As he spoke, Alborn collapsed at Rastín's feet, his hot tears falling on Rastín's hands. "You are your father's son. You are not a specter sent to torment me."

Rastín felt the same, but he did not say so. Instead he waited for Alborn to continue his confession and relieve the burden he carried. "His voice is in my ears…His voice I shall hear always. It is my punishment, the mark of my crime."

"There is no crime in unquestioning loyalty, Alborn son of Jfe. If it was to be done, better you than the alternative."

Alborn sat back on his haunches and found bitterness. "And would you wish the same?"

"If it must be done and if there were no other way, I would." Rastín said it quickly and without hesitation, for he meant every word. "You gave Djerg mercy when no other would. You carry the pain they wished to inflict, but you must let this go now if you're to be of service to me."

"How can the blind and starved be of service to anyone?"

"You have already been of service. When you saw me your first instinct was to protect me, and you've done so."

"My first instinct was to be selfish. I should not have done so for I have played you falsely. There is no place for you here. You must know this. Twice bitter is hope given then snatched away."

"You, dear friend, have listened too long outside my father's door. Your words have his voice in them."

Alborn regained his feet with Rastín's help. Then, while looking without seeing, he said, "As do yours."

CHAPTER FIVE

Rastín's reunion with his people was twice bitter, as Alborn had said it would be, and the approach of morning only made things more dire. Long ago Alborn was granted the right to remain in the camp, and that right had not been revoked. Few of the living had that right, and Rastín was not one of them. If he remained in the camp, and was found out, those who served the ageless would decide his fate. If he left the camp, and was found out, his father's enemies would decide his fate. Either would bring death. But now exhaustion overcame him and he slipped into a deep sleep.

He awoke some tolls later, but well before the sounding of the first toll, to find Alborn preparing what meager fare the old guard could scrounge. He did not doubt Alborn had also added some things he had secreted away previously and had been keeping in case a need arose. He did not want to eat what little remained of the old guard's food, but to refuse would be an insult; so he ate as Alborn sat nearby. He praised the old guard as sincerely and affectionately as he could, because Alborn was all that remained of his father and his past life.

Rastín finished eating. Immediately Alborn stood and said, "I'll escort you to the dig. You'll be safe until you reach the gate and likely while you work. It will be on the return, when word has spread, that you'll need to be on your guard. They will come at you then, whether in the lines or in this camp, and there will be no safe ground until they've killed you or you've won."

Rastín reached forward and clasped hands with the old guard. "There is no need for you to leave camp. No need at all."

Alborn thought otherwise.

"Few others have had the run of this camp and much of the city since our fall," he said carefully. "And though I may not see with my eyes, I am not blind. No other knows this camp as I do. I will deliver you to the gate."

"You will not be able to return and it will mean your—" Rastín's voice dropped off.

The sounding of the first toll spoke for them both. An awkward silence followed until Alborn broke it. "We will wait until much of the camp clears, and then I will take you along the outer path. I carry the sign of the ageless. The guardians will not challenge me, but you must help me do something about my appearance and yours."

Water was one thing they had in abundance, so Rastín helped Alborn clean himself up then did the same. Afterward, Alborn excused himself and went out into the camp.

Alone, there was nothing to keep Rastín's dark thoughts in check. Suddenly, he felt an unbearable weight—the weight of his people and futures lost. He could not breathe. He needed air. He needed to think, but he began to doubt. Many tocks of the toll had passed and Alborn had not returned. Had Alborn betrayed him?

He whirled around at a movement behind him, but it was only Alborn returning with two weather-stained but otherwise good cloaks with hoods. Yet something else was wrapped within the cloaks, which Alborn presented on bended knee. Rastín could not believe his eyes as he lifted the cloaks and saw what was hidden within. He touched the shards as one would touch the most precious jewels.

"Each piece has been carried by one of the loyal these many cycles," Alborn told him. "Though you were born a slave and have never walked the land of our people, I know in my heart that this belongs to you, for you are my king."

"Where? How?" began Rastín, not quite knowing what to say.

"Though few, the loyal remain. When commanded, they act without question. I have asked from them the one thing they hold dearer than their own lives, so you may have it now and be the one to carry it forth for our people. It does not come without burden."

"You have been its keeper through it all?"

"I alone have been the keeper of nothing save your father's will. The others are its true keepers. Accept only if you can give that which can never be reclaimed. Refuse and I must see this returned to those who will carry it for our people. I don't mean to hurry your decision, but the second toll will sound soon and I must know before then."

Alborn knew Rastín had accepted before Rastín ever spoke aloud. On his signal, a young elf maiden entered. She was lithe and slender, like most of his kind, with a well-kept mane of silver. Her skin, bronzed by the suns, seemed to glow, and her overly large gray eyes seemed able to probe hidden depths. "She is Dierá. She will stitch the shards in. Remove your clothes quickly now to the skin. No time for modesty. Her skill is exceptional, and only a true blade will get out what she stitches in."

Rastín did as he was asked. He expected Dierá to stitch the shards into his clothing, but her hands and Alborn's were upon him before he knew what was happening, and the shards were being sown into his flesh. He would have cried out in surprise, and in fact he guessed that he had; but Alborn and perhaps others had a hand or hands over his mouth to muffle his screams.

When it was nearly over and he had recovered enough to see past the pain, Rastín saw that Alborn had indeed been joined by others, the elf maiden Dierá he had been introduced to and two other elf maidens he did not know.

But the ordeal was not over. He was still being held down and Dierá was straddled across his chest sowing in the last shard. When she finished, she pushed herself against him and spoke into his ear of how the shards must be remade. The touch of her body to his was electrifying. It was all he could think about while she pressed against him, and it took the pain from him even as her words wormed their way into the deepest parts of his mind.

The second toll sounded as Dierá moved off him and he was allowed to stand. When he did, he turned angrily to Alborn and asked, "What have you done?"

Alborn touched a hand to Rastín's shoulder and regarded him with eyes that could not see. "I have done what must be done. What your father entrusted me to do."

Without a word, Dierá helped Rastín dress. "What of them?"

"What of them," Alborn said. "Their fathers knew I would not ask if there was not need, for I have never asked when there was not need. They live or die with you now. Command them to stop breathing and they will die before dishonoring you by taking a breath. Command them to cut out the other's heart and they will do so though they will all three perish."

Rastín threw his hands up in the air even as Dierá was pulling his cloak into place. "Send them back. I have no need for such."

"A choice has been made. It cannot be unmade. Do you not know shieldmaidens when you see them?"

"They are too young. Why would such be needed in this place?"

"In this place ever is the need. Your father kept too much from you to keep you safe, and now there is no time to explain. We must go and we must do so now. Dierá, Eldri, and Síari are yours. Do with them as you will."

"I—"

"Stay to my right, follow my lead. Tell Dierá, Eldri, and Síari to stay ahead of us, no more than a stride away." Alborn started to leave the tent, but as Rastín had not relayed the order, he paused. "I have given them to you. You must command them to act. They will listen to no other."

"Your act makes me no better than the ageless."

Alborn wheeled around; and if Rastín had not known the old guard's eyes were empty sockets, he would have sworn the old guard was not only able to see him but to look into his soul. "Free will is what separates us. They gave themselves freely."

Waving everyone out of the tent, Alborn said, "We'll stay to the outer path, take the northernmost corridor to the gate. After the gate, we'll head to the highlands. Any other that comes within a pace of his highness is to be dealt with."

Rastín turned to the three. "Do as Alborn asks. It is my wish."

Dierá, Eldri, and Síari acquiesced. They left the tent first, moving directly toward the outer path. Alborn and Rastín followed, both with the hoods of their cloaks raised. Rastín carried Alborn's walking stick though he knew the guardians would not allow him to pass through the gates with it.

Alborn set the pace, for he could not move too swiftly, while the shieldmaidens walked an almost courtly pace to stay within a stride. As he walked, Rastín's thoughts swam with images of his father, his mother, the old guard, and the she-beast. In this confused state, he felt that he was both Élvemere and Wërg. In his mind's eye, he was a young Elf who trembled as he stood before his father. His father was telling him to find calm and resolve, and not to show anguish, sorrow, or fear.

Before his mother he was a boy who little understood her deepening despair and angst. His mother was telling him she was leaving for the blessed land where her heart lived. Before Alborn he was the prince of a lost people. The old guard was telling him that his father had joined his mother in the blessed land.

Before Akharran he was Wërg but not Wërg. The she-beast was telling him there was danger, great danger, and that he must now remember. It was the only time the she-beast had called him by his full name—a rare moment in which he felt that he truly was Rastín Dnyarr Túrring of the Élvemere people.

Alborn's hand squeezing his elbow returned Rastín to conscious thought. They were leaving the camp now, going into the heart of the city on their way to the transition corridors and the gate. Ahead, Dierá, Eldri, and Síari had stopped, but Rastín did not know why. Alborn seemed to sense that something was wrong, however, because he too stopped abruptly.

Rastín saw them then: serpent magi, walking within protective lines of overlords flanked by enforcers. Their two great horns and their long muscular torsos on serpent bodies were unmistakable. Like most, these were golden in color with black scales except for a patch of crimson in front. Outside his father's pavilion, he had never seen serpent magi so this sighting was unusual, yet it was made even more so because he was not seeing one or two magi—he was seeing many, all headed toward the transition corridors and the thousand-fold gates.

Alborn did not hesitate long. At his first step Rastín followed, as did Dierá, Eldri, and Síari, but the shieldmaidens instinctively took different positions. Dierá, a stride ahead, kept to the left. Eldri and Síari, a stride behind, kept to the right.

With his training as the son of a king, Rastín understood this flanking formation. Dierá kept the path ahead clear. Eldri and Síari ensured no one could attack him from behind. Rastín doubted anyone's attentions were on him, however, as the appearance of the serpent magi was unsettling and sure to be the focus of anyone nearby. Their presence certainly was the focus of *his* thoughts, and all he could think about was Akharran warning him of danger, great danger.

CHAPTER SIX

Rastín grabbed Alborn's arm and pulled him into a dark recess where a large drainage pipe emptied sewage from the towers above. He was not surprised when Dierá, Eldri, and Síari followed and quietly melded into the shadows. He started to speak, to question the old guard, but paused, remembering his encounter with Akharran in a similar place. After a few heartbeats without speaking, he finally asked, "Have you ever seen anything such as this?"

Alborn regarded Rastín. "Tell me what it is you see."

"Overlords, enforcers, magi. More than can be counted."

Alborn put his right hand on Rastín's shoulder. "No, see without seeing and tell me what it is that you see."

"Now is not the time to speak with my father's voice, Alborn. There is no—"

"There is always time. You think that because I have no eyes that I do not see, yet I see. I see with clarity beyond yours. Your vision is as clouded as your thoughts. Our people need a king and yet on this day you are not that king, nor can you be, but you are my king as you are

Dierá's, Eldri's, and Síari's."

Alborn continued before Rastín could speak. "You have never seen because you do not see. Djerg and I have stood ever vigilant outside your father's door, and yet you did not see us. You see only what you think you ought to see.

"In your eyes I am no more than Alborn, son of Jfe, a guard at your father's service. I am no more such than Dierá is a naïve elf maiden. You say you hear your father's voice in my words, yet what if my voice was in your father's words?"

From the shadows, Dierá looked urgently at Rastín. Time was short. Rastín turned back to Alborn and said, "Twice you spoke of my return as if I were away and you knew I was coming back."

"Did you think it was by chance that you came to be among the Wërg or that by chance the Wërg queen chose you? Nothing happens to the son of the High King by chance. Not in this place or any other. Nothing."

"I did not think. I did not understand. Was Akharran their queen?"

"You do not know kings from shieldmaidens when they stand before you. I warned your father about keeping so much from you."

Rastín grew quiet as he reflected on all Alborn had said. "If only there was time for you to teach me all that must be taught."

Further talk was cut short when Dierá stepped from the shadows. "We must go now," she said. "Eldri and Síari will follow."

Returning to the corridor and seeing the thinning traffic, Rastín knew at once why Dierá had urged him to continue on. Certainly, passing tardily through the gates would make them stand out more than if they were part of the main flow.

Rastín drummed his fingers against the walking stick he carried for Alborn, glancing back over his shoulder to Eldri and Síari. The two were even younger than Dierá, who could not be more than sixty winters old. For elf kind, it meant they were little more than children as he himself was little more than an adolescent with thirty cycles to go before his centennial and adulthood. And yet his burden was their burden.

He searched his soul, but he did not know with a certainty what he should do. Alborn's plan had been so simple: Leave the tent, follow the outer path out of the camp, take the northernmost corridor to the gate, go through the gate and into the highlands. But *then* what? If the work in the dark land did not kill Alborn by midday, they still would not be able to work within half of chain of each other, and with that much separation there was no way the shieldmaidens could protect him.

At the gate, Rastín meant to push the walking stick into Alborn's hands and turn him back toward the camp. He knew it was a foolish thought. The old guard did have the mark of right, and the chances were good the guardians would let Alborn return without question. Rastín never got the chance, however, as one of the gate's guardians snatched the walking stick out of his hands before he could pass it to Alborn. He heard Dierá take the whips meant for him, but Alborn edged him into the gate behind Eldri and Síari.

In the bitter cold, in the place between places, Rastín tasted something he had never tasted before. He tasted cynicism and found doubt, but not his own. Then he saw Akharran as clearly as he had ever seen her, yet this was not the Akharran he had known. This was an Akharran that moved with the skill of a hunter, and she hunted him.

When he emerged into the dark land, he saw Eldri and Síari ahead of him on the platform. Mere steps later he felt Alborn by his side. As he glanced over to regard Alborn, he saw Dierá, her fixed eyes spoke to him. Inside she was full of anger, and that anger was directed at him, but outside she was composed and focused.

Rastín joined the right flank of the lines moving to the excavation site with Eldri positioned in front of him, Síari to his left, Dierá behind him, and Alborn to his right. The jagged mountains where they would dig were a league or more distant. During the long march, the lines always broke up, but for now the overlords kept them in tight formation.

Away from the thousand-fold gates, he began to see formations with overlords, enforcers, and serpent magi. Alborn became agitated whenever the magi were close, and it was so uncharacteristic that Rastín finally said, "You know why they are here, don't you?"

"I told your father the Wërg were a poor choice. He believed their promises, yet I thought otherwise."

Rastín grew quiet as he reflected on all that Alborn had told him since his return. "I must be a great disappointment to you, but I will make you a promise. While I live, I will carry the burdens and hopes of our people. Though our paths surely must part soon, I will strive to my last breath to become for all our people the king that you so wished to see in me."

Alborn stopped walking abruptly, breaking formation. They were far enough away from both the gates and the dig site that the closest overlord would dismiss it—or at least Rastín hoped that would be the case.

"In your heart, Rastín, I know you believe this. As I promised your father, I have done what I could. I could not save Djerg, but I believe in my heart that I can save our people if I can save you."

At the approach of an overlord, Rastín helped Alborn start walking. Dierá, Eldri, and Síari joined step with them. Rastín waited for the overlord to pass by, and then said, "You tell me nothing happens to the son of the High King by chance. You tell me I do not see, that I would not know a king from a shieldmaiden. You tell me that I am your king, and yet what is a king to a king."

"Rastín, now is not the time for this discussion. You will see when you remember. Despite your fears to the contrary, I will make it through this day's labor—it is the night I worry about."

"The night?" Rastín cast his eyes to the distance. He saw only the jagged mountains and the places where the night criers lived.

"We've long known this place is habitable. There is water and game and life beyond—"

"—nothing lives beyond."

"A careful balance exists between predator and prey, as in all things. You can't know this, as you were not among the first workers; but the night criers nearly outnumbered us before the ageless culled them, turning beasts of prey into beasts of burden."

Several chains ahead, Rastín saw workers lining up in formations thousands across. High overhead, the overlords formed their own lines. These things in and of themselves were odd, but when the overlords' staffs of office began transforming into fiery whips and those whips began lashing out at the masses, panic spread throughout the lines.

Workers scattered, running in every direction. Those who did not move quickly enough were being trampled. Dierá, Eldri, and Síari formed a protective circle around Rastín and Alborn. Then the sky cracked and lightning fell through, carrying with it black smoke and ash.

Alborn was the most calm. He drew himself up, releasing his grip on Rastín's arm. His steady gaze led Rastín's eyes beyond the overlords to the magi who were calling forth the lightning. Alborn spoke then, quietly yet urgent. "Do not put their lives above yours. As long as our people live and the faithful remain, there is no death for them, only renewal of the flesh."

Rastín thought Alborn spoke of the dying but soon realized Alborn's words were for Eldri and Síari, who were already seriously injured. Síari held in her guts with one hand while she bravely fought with her other arm, using her legs when her arm alone was not enough.

"We move now, to the mountains," Alborn said urgently, and without hesitation Dierá, Eldri, and Síari began to carve a path ahead. Rastín broken into a run, moving as fast as Alborn could move and the panic allowed.

Thousands of others were already well ahead of them, racing into the dig site to find cover or open space where the lightning would not find them. Little did they realize they were being herded into this place by the overlords and the magi.

Rastín had run fewer than three chains when the lighting stopped just as suddenly as it had begun. Then the overlords called out with one voice—that of the ageless—to the workers. "There will be finds this day, and one of those finds will be the cornerstone we seek. Fail us and this will be your last day in this life, for we will no longer have need for you."

"Paradox," Alborn said as he collapsed to his haunches. The look on the old guard's face was of such exhaustion that Rastín feared the other was taking his last breaths. "If true, we are dead either way."

"Then we will hope they lie, as ever," Rastín muttered as he squatted down next to Alborn. His next thoughts were of Dierá, Eldri, and Síari as he watched them tend each other's wounds. Removing his cloak, he began tearing off long strips for bandages. Several of these long strips were needed to hold in Síari's entrails.

Finishing, Rastín bowed his head. Cloaks or no cloaks, other elves had recognized both Rastín and Alborn during the panicked run. Word was spreading among the Élvemere that the son of the high king lived. He must think and act appropriately now more than ever if he wanted to live. He knew any mistake could cost his own life as well as the lives of Dierá, Eldri, Síari, and Alborn. As order was restored, he also knew they had precious little time to decide a course of action.

CHAPTER SEVEN

Like armies of buzzers pouring forth from their underground nests, the peoples of a hundred worlds spread across the mountainside. Work resumed, and with it the familiar din of pick and ax biting into rock. Rastín paced and cursed, finally breaking the long silence by asking, "Alborn, you must know. What is it I must do? Is there something I can do?"

Dierá, Eldri, and Síari remained quiet. They knew the question was directed at Alborn. For his part, Alborn regarded Rastín with eyes that could not see but somehow did. He did not speak for some time. In those silent moments Rastín again was certain the old guard was seeing beyond flesh and bone. "If escape into the highlands will not be possible come nightfall, we must look for another way. For now, though, it seems we must dig and pray."

"Pray to what? The ageless dogs? There is nothing left to discover."

"Perhaps," Alborn said. "Or perhaps it could be that it was found and forgotten."

Rastín shouldered a discarded pick and ax. Eldri and Síari did likewise. Dierá set off by herself across the dig site and returned with picks and axes for herself and Alborn.

As before when they marched, Dierá, Eldri, and Síari moved out from Rastín's current position in a protective pattern. Dierá began digging a chain to his left. Eldri moved a chain up the mountain. Síari moved a chain to his right. The three heaved their picks and thrust them against the barren rock of the mountain almost in unison, and the echoes of this activity joined the growing din.

Alborn found a spot a chain below Rastín that had already been partially dug out by another. Rastín slammed the tooth of the pick into the ground at his own feet, rock chips and dust flying in every direction. The steady rhythm of the labor kept his mind occupied for a time. Heave, thrust, crunch. Heave, thrust, crunch.

In the first toll, he looked up from his work only once, so he could check on Alborn. The old guard, although clearly tired, was holding his own. Seeing this pleased Rastín. For a time afterward, Rastín only knew the rhythm of heave, thrust, and crunch; the sweat beading on his brow and dripping down his back; the cool, light wind off the mountains.

The overlords, serpent magi, and even the ageless became as nothing to him, because they were outside, beyond the place where the work carried him. He had spent cycles of his life in this place with only the rhythm to keep him company. Without the soothing rhythm there was nothing. Within, everything.

Many tolls passed, lost to the rhythm. It was nearly midday when Rastín returned to conscious thoughts, and he only did so because as he looked up from the pit he created a Wërg stood over him. The Wërg was piling rock and earth. Her carts were half filled.

Looking up at the Wërg, he could not help but read her expression. She was telling him, "Danger, great danger. Dny must now remember." When she told him this, Rastín was certain she was Akharran.

"Promises not kept," he told her, using her language. "Father dead."

"Death," Akharran replied. "Great death."

Rastín was uncertain whether she was speaking of his father's death or something else, but he did not have time to dwell on it. The midday reprieve was called, and Akharran was forced to depart hastily.

Each in turn, Dierá, Eldri, and Síari moved off to get food and water, each returning with an extra share that was meant for Rastín and Alborn. But when Rastín tried to eat or drink, the food and water were pulled away. "We eat, you wait," Dierá told him.

Rastín did not understand. Alborn explained, saying quietly, "They check for taint. If they do not become sick, the food and water are safe."

"I do not like this new life," Rastín told Alborn plainly. "What am I that my own people would poison and kill me?"

"It is what it is, what it has been since the reckoning and before. A high king is appointed, rather than crowned. You must know this, although I know your father kept much from you.

"Our fractured people have forgotten much. They have forgotten the kings of old, and now hold only to petty rivalry as each great house and each great family struggles to rise up and claim thrones of a land that is no more.

"Élvemere is gone, Rastín. It is ash and dust. Only your father kept the memory alive. For in him, the dream, the wish that is

Élvemere lived. Without him, Élvemere is nothing. Gone, lost. We are a people made vagrant. We have no land, no home; and even the dream, the wish, the memory is now gone."

When Dierá signaled it was all right for Rastín to eat and drink, he and Alborn commenced.

Alborn continued, "Much more than you dare to guess is at hand. In this place, the future of everyone and everything will be decided. I am certain your father spoke to you of this thing that we unearth. Tell me, Rastín Dnyarr Túrring, of this thing that has taken our people and claimed our beloved Élvemere."

Remembering now a thing from the past, Rastín drew himself up, his steady gaze never leaving Alborn's face. He was about to answer, but instead said, "Élvemere lives. Whether it is wish or dream, it lives because I say it does. It lives in me. Although others may call themselves king, our people have but one high king. I am he as was my father before me."

Alborn stood beside Rastín. "You are my king. If you say Élvemere lives, who am I to question otherwise? By your stance, I take it you have remembered now a thing found and then forgotten. You have a decision to make, Rastín Dnyarr Túrring. A choice must be made."

Síari regarded Rastín, and Rastín in turn could not help but notice how wounds had bled through the bandages. Her face was pale and there were deepening circles under her eyes. But there was a light in her eyes and a smile on her lips. As he watched her, she took in a breath, exhaled; took in a breath, exhaled. Then she closed her eyes and was no more.

Death was no stranger to Rastín. In this place, Rastín had seen more death in the short cycles of his life than most elves see in the long millennia of their long lives, yet Síari's death moved him to tears, carried away words he meant to speak, and swept him to his knees.

Certainly, he had wept openly upon hearing of his father's death, but he had never before found tears such as these. In that moment, he could not have explained why Síari's death affected him so; indeed even later when he reflected on that moment he could not say with a certainty why he had broken down in great fits and sobs.

Perhaps it was a sudden understanding of the burden he carried or what his failures meant. Regardless of cause, Rastín Dnyarr Túrring rose from bended knee a king in his hearts of hearts—and not a king because others said he was a king, a king because he knew it through to his soul. From this day forward, no matter what was done to him, he promised himself he would never not be a king.

He touched a hand then to Alborn's shoulder. The old guard seemed to know what Rastín would do next even if Rastín himself did not know. Just before he turned and walked away, Rastín said, "I see without seeing. I know without knowing. You have done right by my family, and one day I hope to do right by you. Dierá and Eldri are yours now. They will keep you and serve you as they would me."

CHAPTER EIGHT

Fire and lightning rained down from blood-red skies to mark the end of the midday reprieve. Rastín paid this no heed as he trudged across the mountainside, moving among the pits, searching.

It was a toll passed midday when he found it. Plain enough. A pit not unlike all the others before it. Ten spans deep and twenty spans across. He climbed in, called out to the heavens.

At first there was no answer, and so Rastín called out again and then again before there came a response. In a great pouring forth, his people came. They came not because he was their king, but because he had cried out to the heavens and because his words told of a discovery.

He worked then among countless thousands until the great gray stone was unearthed and revealed. As he stood there, looking up at the heavens, he knew blessed death would come. He was ready to receive this gift, as ready as he had ever been.

A hundred overlords descended from the heavens, walked down living stairs and living carpets to stand before him. Behind the overlords came ever more serpent magi. Soon there was no place

Rastín could look to see the eyes of his kind.

Forced to his knees to accept the blessed gift, Rastín saw Holsteb and endless lines of those who had been blessed before him, their faces looming before his eyes as in life. As Síari had done at the last, he took in a breath, exhaled; took in a breath, exhaled. Then he closed his eyes and prepared to become no more.

As one, the overlords touched the tips of their staffs to his head and imparted the gift of the ageless. Behind the overlords, the magi chanted and exalted him. Lightning flashed from the heavens then, one hundred bolts, and every worker and every beast in every corner of the dark land paid tribute to the exaltation by crying out.

Rastín's own screams joined those wailing his praises as lightning rent flesh from bone. Pain became so excruciating that Rastín felt it was all he had ever known. Then there was blackness so deep, cold, and remote that he would never again think of the place between places as dark or cold or lonely.

He awoke from this blackness lost within himself, unsure of anything, void of everything, save the knowledge that he had been exalted when he had wished for nothing more than blessed parting. His sight was the first of his senses to return, though the world before him was blurred and obscured. Hearing followed, making him wish he had not ears. He heard only the sounds of the damned, issuing forth in wave after wave.

With those sounds, he knew he was within the great towers that breathed fire and vented smoke and ash. Indeed, as smell, taste, and touch returned, they seemed to bear him out. His last thought before slipping back into unconsciousness was that if he was exalted, he had not been given the choice of companion that all the others before him had been given.

The press of warm flesh close to his own should have been enough to tell him otherwise. Consciously or not, he had chosen Dierá. He awoke many tolls later to the young shieldmaiden tending to him with attentive care and an affection he had not known she was capable of.

Clearly she was pleased to see him rouse, and even more pleased when he was able to sit. She fed him then, scraps of bread, watery soup, as had been pushed under the door some tolls before.

"You do not know this," she said quietly, "but our fathers chose us for each other long before either of us were born. In Élvemere, I was to have been a queen, your wife, your beloved. I was bred to this as you were bred to be a king.

"In this place, it is us who must breed. It is what the magi have told me; the reason for you to choose me."

Rastín pushed away, putting his back to the cool, damp wall of the cell. "Are we in the great towers that breathe fire?"

"I think so, though what lies beyond this door you do not wish to see."

"How did you come to be in this place?"

Dierá hung her head. "When you were taken to stand before the magi, you chose me, though you may not remember. Some time has passed since your great find."

"M-m-my great find?" Rastín started to remember. Somewhere far off he thought he heard music. It seemed an age since he had heard music.

"You found the missing cornerstone, the last cornerstone. The magi were greatly pleased and yet displeased, because they were certain the find was kept from them. It is good that you do not know this time."

Rastín gripped Dierá's shoulders. "How much time has passed?"

"Truly I do not know. I've lost track of time since."

"Before you were taken to the towers?" Rastín asked, squeezing her shoulders with more force than he intended.

Dierá's expression told him that his grip pained her, though she said not a word of this. "Some tendays passed…" Her voice trailed off, then she added, "It is better that you do not know this time."

As his vision cleared and his other senses returned fully, he saw she was covered with welts and bruises. He released her and sat back, but she pushed herself up against him.

A voice from the darkness said, "A slave is nothing if not another's play thing." Rastín recognized his favorite language, Jurin. He loved its harshness on the tongue, and in particular the harshness of its curses.

Fire lit behind Rastín's eyes at the hearing, and he suddenly was alert and lunging into the darkness, certain that the one behind this voice had hurt Dierá. He barely managed a ten-stride however, before he collapsed. Dierá helped him back to their corner of the dark cell.

"Your fire is why the masters have kept you," said the voice, "My fire, my curse." As the other said this, the darkness was cleared, lit by living fires.

Rastín rarely saw the mammoth ones in the dark land or the immortal city, but he knew who and what they were. "You are…"

"We are Empyrjurin, as you are Élvemere."

"Your fire, I thought you bore it always."

Crouching, because he could not stand, the gargant moved toward Rastín. "As I'm sure you are certain, Styrjurin bore wind and Fhurjurin bore earth and stone. However, do you think we eat with fire ever burning in the oils of our flesh?"

Remembering the harshness of the Jurin curses, which spoke of grinding bone, tearing flesh, spilling entrails, and much more, Rastín was certain he and Dierá were in danger. "I am exalted," he said, his voice booming. "You will keep your distance."

The gargant's laughter boomed from the ceiling. Rastín did not understand what was so funny and so he hurled the foulest of his foul curses at the gargant. The gargant's response was laughter that shook the floor.

In Elvish, Dierá said, "They are friends."

"They?" questioned Rastín even as he finally discerned faces among the many fires spread throughout the enormous cell.

"Without G'rkyr, I would not be here. Nor would you."

"G'rkyr?"

"I am G'rkyr," the gargant said, half crouching, half crawling closer. "And switching to Elvish is very impolite. I told you that I can still understand you, as can Zanük; but the others, they cannot."

Looking up at the gargant with his great bold eyes, his knuckles dragging across the floor, and his neck bent against the ceiling, Rastín felt as if the walls of the cell were closing in on them. Surely it was only a matter of moments before they were all crushed to death. As the gargant reached out to him, he felt a heart-sized lump well up in his throat. This feeling of walls closing in only worsened when the others of G'rkyr's kind crawled closer.

"The little one peeping out behind G'rkyr is Zanük," Dierá said. "They are inseparable except when it comes to their curiosity of us little folk, and then Zanük cowers behind G'rkyr. Isn't that right, Zanük?"

"I do not," Zanük protested, his voice deep and loud.

Rastín's eyes grew wide as Zanük moved from behind G'rkyr. Zanük was anything but little, nearly a third bigger than G'rkyr; and G'rkyr was huge.

"They are Three Hammers clan," Dierá murmured to Rastín. "The ageless have declared war on their people. It is their reckoning day, and may the Great Mother watch over theirs."

G'rkyr said, "I hear you, little one, even when you whisper."

"Ha!" Dierá said, "I'm not whispering. Sometimes we little folk like to talk quietly among ourselves. We do not need our voices to boom and rumble to prove ourselves."

Rastín saw there was something unsaid between Dierá and G'rkyr, perhaps an old argument to which he was not privy. He did not, however, have the energy or focus to follow fully their banter, and he could not help himself when his eyelids drooped and closed.

He heard Dierá shoo the curious giantfolk back. "When we did not breed, we were put here among the Empyrjurin."

"Put here?" Rastín asked.

"As food," the gargant said.

"Not as food," Dierá countered as she scolded the gargant. "G'rkyr's belly is the focus of his thoughts—all too often. I'm surprised little Zanük still has arms, and that G'rkyr has not eaten them while his brother slept." Switching to Elvish, she added, "The masters meant us as gifts."

"Elf kind are gifts to giantfolk?"

"Tasty gifts," G'rkyr said; and for this Dierá swatted the gargant's nose, but she had to jump up in the air to do so.

"G'rkyr is the one who figured out how to bring you to

consciousness. You'll have to forgive his petulance, for he is ever jealous of my regard for you."

"But I am exalted," Rastín said, his voice booming again.

"Lies," Dierá said, "All lies. The blessed are brought here. They are not cleansed or raised to the blessed land. Here, they are as the masters wish it…"

"Food or entertainment. Sometimes both," added G'rkyr with a knowing relish that made Rastín shrink back. Dierá chased G'rkyr away by swatting his nose a few more times.

"What of the exalted? Surely there must be reward," Rastín asked.

"Of a certainty," Dierá said, and then she repeated it, but would say no more.

CHAPTER NINE

Days passed before Rastín felt strong enough to do anything other than sit idly and talk with Dierá, G'rkyr, and the other Empyrjurin sharing the cavernous cell. At times Dierá, G'rkyr, and others would be summoned out of the cell. When Dierá returned, she would always go directly to one of the open cisterns along the southerly wall and bathe before joining Rastín. He never dared ask why.

While Dierá bathed, she sang. Her voice carried well. It was as beautiful and haunting as the songs she chose. Most were ballads that told of battles lost, the death of the great ones, and the final days of Élvemere. Rastín's second self was always keenly aware of the songs and their words, even if his other self in the waking world paid them little attention.

G'rkyr used these opportunities to batter Rastín with stinging banter or open mocking. The gargant had taken to calling Rastín "Exalted" or "His Empirical Majestic Exalted One." Rastín knew the gargant had no idea that Rastín was actually a prince among elf kind, but these and other quips only made Rastín increasingly resentful of G'rkyr and the other giantfolk.

As G'rkyr began this day's tirade, Rastín looked up at the gargant with indifferent eyes. His expression told the gargant his thoughts.

In response, G'rkyr took his huge finger and jabbed Rastín in the gut, making Rastín double over. As the gargant did this, he said, "Remember, Exalted, you are here only because she would not leave you and begged me to find a way to help you."

Hoping to avoid goading the gargant on, Rastín said, "I was told I have you to thank for this. On behalf of my people, the Élvemere, I thank you."

"Your people, your people. His Empirical Majestic Exalted One sure is fond of himself. You think I swept you from dream and shadow willingly? That one—" G'rkyr pointed to Dierá as she bathed "—has the ftokish tongue."

"I hear you," Dierá called out.

Rastín grinned. The word *ftokish* was a vulgarism particular to the southerly region of Jurin where G'rkyr's clan lived. The closest Rastín had ever come to understanding its meaning was through Dierá's reaction to it. He suspected he would understand all the Empyrjurin idioms and vulgarisms in time—or at least those used by the Three Hammers clan. Still, it irked him that Dierá and G'rkyr had such a strong connection.

Rather than stay and argue with the gargant, Rastín went to a place he knew the other would not dare to go. He went to the cisterns where Dierá bathed and sang the saddest song he had ever heard. The elf maiden did not shy away from him. Instead she finished her song and then asked, "You have decided, then?"

"I have decided nothing," Rastín replied as he sat.

"Do you find me unattractive or unsuitable in some way?"

He regarded her, taking in the deep bronze of her bare shoulders, the long line of her neck, the perfect oval of her face, the roundness of her gray eyes, and the silver of her hair in a single, lingering glance. "You are beautiful," he told her, and he meant it. "But I will not do this thing because they command it."

Dierá stood and walked from the cistern. Her naked form drew Rastín's eyes as was her intention. Her breasts were not as full as some, but they were pleasing. Both round and firm. Her slender waist accentuated the curve of her hips. Her backside was shapely, and she turned to ensure he saw this. "Then do this thing for me," she said as she leaned down to him.

At her touch and at the press of her lips against his, Rastín felt his desire rise. He could not help this, but he could not allow himself to continue. Dierá had twice been given to him—once by his own people and once by the ageless—though for different reasons. It was all the same, and all meant to sink him to a level of depravity where the ageless owned not only his life but his soul. Though his life might be forfeit, Rastín decided his soul was his own, and for this reason he gently pushed Dierá away. One day, if Dierá came to him of her own free will, things would be different, but that day was not today.

Across the cell, G'rkyr applauded and jeered, causing Rastín to charge with a ferocity that surprised the gargant. As G'rkyr landed on his backside, smashing his head against the low ceiling, Rastín's charge ended with a flying leap as he kicked out at the gargant's chest with both feet. The gargant fell flat on his back with Rastín straddled across his neck.

"Mock me now," Rastín said as he choked the gargant, squeezing with his legs and hands. "I dare you."

G'rkyr, for all his size and might, had never suspected Rastín was capable of knocking him down, let alone trying to choke the wind out of him. G'rkyr flailed about, trying to knock Rastín off; but Rastín only tightened his grip.

Having slipped on her light shift, Dierá stalked across the cell until she was standing at G'rkyr's shoulder. "G'rkyr, Rastín does not understand that you mock him because of your fondness for me. He can be as thick-headed and single-minded as you!"

Pulling Rastín off the gargant, she said, "Rastín, I am as fond of G'rkyr as he is of me."

Rastín's expression spoke of the incredulity he was feeling. "You have feelings for a gargant?"

"I do indeed," Dierá said, kissing G'rkyr's cheek and helping him sit up.

G'rkyr smiled and gloated.

"Have your gargant, then!" Rastín shouted, throwing his hands up in the air and walking away. As he moved to the opposite side of the cell, the other Empyrjurin shied away from him. Preferring the company of Dierá and G'rkyr to his, they left him alone. Even Zanük, G'rkyr's closest rival, would not speak to Rastín.

Dierá sulked for the rest of the day. When the dinner cauldrons were brought in, Dierá served Rastín as ever. However, instead of handing him the bowl of stewed meat, she shoved it at him, causing much of it to spill. "Do eat what is on the floor," she told him as she stalked away. "Otherwise, you are likely to get hungry in the night."

"Dierá," he called after her. "It doesn't have to be like this. I'm sorry. Sit by me."

Obediently, Dierá sat where she stood, refusing to look at him.

Frustrated, Rastín walked over to her. "You do not have to sit if you do not want to sit."

"Oh, but I do," Dierá told him quietly, bitterly.

G'rkyr looked up from his bowl, started to grunt something. Rastín ignored the gargant as he knelt next to Dierá. "If this is how you will be, then I free you. You are free, I tell you. Go. From now on, I shall be as nothing to you and you shall be as nothing to me."

Dierá mocked him then, much as G'rkyr had done earlier, and her scorn cut him more deeply than any blade ever could. "'I free you,'" she laughed, mimicking his movements and expression. "*You* free *me*…Ha! Have you ever in your life considered your words before they came out of your mouth? Have you ever thought of anyone else beside yourself? Have you ever truly seen what is right before your eyes? Do you understand nothing?"

Her large eyes were so wild and angry that G'rkyr and the other Empyrjurin turned away from them. Yet as she spoke, Rastín could tell that Dierá knew that every word was wrong and that every word cut at his heart, but she seemed unable to stop herself. It seemed he was there and those she wished were in his place were not, so she raged and she raged.

"I was to have been your queen, your wife, your beloved. I was to be the air you breathe, the water you drink, the light of your eyes. I can never be free of you though you, without a care, wish to be free of me. How dare you!

"And how dare you take out your anger on G'rkyr? Do you not see that he is more child than adult? As are they all."

Rastín looked past Dierá to the hulking mass of gargants clustered tightly on the far side of the cell. Most were half crouching with their heads bent over. In this position, their fisted hands touched the floor. Although he looked and looked, Rastín could not see youth.

"If G'rkyr and the others were adults, they would not be here with us. You do not understand what it means for the masters—" Dierá used the gargant's word for the ageless. "—to make us gifts to them. We have known nothing save lies. Go beyond the doors of this cell. You will see the truth of it all. You will pray to your mother in the blessed land then. You will pray for one such as G'rkyr.

"When all others had forsaken us, G'rkyr dared befriend me. G'rkyr kept me alive in the masters' halls when so many others were not as fortunate. The masters' halls are places beyond horror—beyond the horrors of your worst imaginings."

Dierá pounded her fists against Rastín's chest, but it did nothing to slow her angry outpouring. "Oh, it would all be so much simpler if you would just do what the masters wish. It is why they punish us and make us a gift to the Empyrjurin. Why can you not do this one thing? Why can you not do this one thing for me? You said I was beautiful. Are your words as full of lies as theirs?"

As she pounded and pounded her fists, her words became increasingly hateful and wrathful. She blamed Rastín for anything and everything that had ever happened to her and hers. She blamed Rastín's father for his failures on the day of reckoning. She cursed the House of Túrring. She vowed to kill him in his sleep. She cried out until she was spent and there was nothing left but fitful sobs.

Although Rastín's heart was cold because of all the hateful, loathsome things she said, he held her. They remained thus, with her at his feet and him hunched over, holding her, through the long tolls of the night. While she slept, he lay awake whispering the words he wished he had had the courage to say earlier. "I see you, Dierá," he told her as she slept. "I see you and I find your beauty beyond anything I had ever dreamed. You have beauty in your heart and in your face and in your form. Hate me, curse me, if you now must, but I know now for a certainty my father chose well.

"I forgive all you have done in my name. I thank you from the bottom of my heart. You kept me when there was no other. You held faith when no other would. And yet I could not, cannot, do the one thing you so wish.

"You do not understand that this thing you wish can never be. It is simply another lie, another way to control, another way to bend and break us. Alborn understood. He helped me see the truth within the lies. I am a king, Dierá, I feel it in my heart, but I have no land and no people save you now. And what will happen to this dream, to this wish that is Élvemere. Does it die with us? Or has it already died within us and we are as yet afraid to say that it is so?

"In Élvemere, you would have been my queen—you would have been the High Queen. Our people would have loved you as I would have loved you. But this is not, nor will it ever be, Élvemere. I have lain with Wërg—the beast people—and I am ashamed to say I did not dislike it. At times I feel that I am Wërg, Dierá, and at these times Élvemere is not even a dream in my heart."

Drawing back her hair from her face, he whispered a promise into her ear, "Whatever comes of this defiance, I take upon myself."

In the morning, Rastín and Dierá were called out. Dierá's tears and sobs began anew as they followed a chained and manacled slave of a winged and horned race Rastín had never seen before. As the cell door closed G'rkyr held out a burning hand to them, but neither saw this. Rastín's attentions were on Dierá, for she was in such a state that it took everything he had just to keep her moving.

"Tell me of the songs you sing?" he asked her, to change her focus.

At first he thought she did not hear him, for his voice was very soft, and then she said in hushed tones, "They are songs of Élvemere lost."

Through the eyes of his father, Rastín had traveled to many lands and feasted in the halls of many kings. But those experiences hardly prepared him for the great hall of the masters, with its ceiling lost from view in shadow and its walls so far off that it seemed he walked in a chamber without walls. Yet it was not so much the hall itself as what was in the hall that made his stomach churn and his heart pound. Here the ageless walked.

Before this day, before this very moment, Rastín would have sworn that he would have gone to the blessed land before ever seeing a living ageless. For in his mind the ageless were the never seen, and yet there they were—everywhere as far as the eye could see—and they were more terrible, more horrendous to behold than his worst imaginings.

The winged and horned one had been silent as he hurried Rastín and Dierá along dark pathways and up stairs; but as they raced along a curbed path behind a table of impossible dimensions, the creature spoke.

"Slaves must keep within the slave runs. Slaves do not deign to look upon their masters. It is not for slaves to behold unless beheld. It is not for slaves to speak unless spoken to."

Rastín cast his eyes down and concentrated on quieting Dierá, yet he could not shake the images of the mammoth, scaly darkspawn he had seen. In many ways they appeared both humanoid and lizardlike, yet each had a pair of great wings protruding from its back and thick spikes longer than he was tall along the shoulders, arms, and tail. He was certain these were the ageless. Although he knew he should fear them as Dierá did, he did not, for if they were truly of flesh and bone, they were no longer the dark whisperers who walked veiled in shadow.

The winged and horned one whirled around and cast his weighted chain at Rastín. "It is not for slaves to decide whether their masters are of flesh and bone."

Rastín dodged the chain easily and without a thought, but the creature's words caused him to retreat within his second self. It was from this place, once removed from the world, that he came face to face with the great king of the ageless—a behemoth who sat a colossal gilded throne like any two-legged creature might, yet his shape was that of a great, grave winged and armored caiman covered in thick scales, long claws, and curved horns.

The back of the throne was open at the bottom to accommodate the thick tail with its pairs of spikes that projected sideways and ran partway up its length as well. His head with its enormous rounded muzzle and great black spheres for eyes was monstrous and crowned with an elongated crest of burnished scales and curved horns that were ringed from base to tip. The gaping maw filled with razor sharp teeth had oversized canines, and below this an apron of thick bones embedded in the scales protected the throat.

Even as the great king of the ageless spread his barbed wings wide, and his guide and Dierá cowered on their knees, Rastín stood as if in his father's hall. His head was bowed, as he was outwardly tending to Dierá even while contemplating all that was before him.

His stance made the ageless king laugh loudly and raucously. "Impenitent, unabashed little bit of nothing," the king said as he reached out and picked up Rastín.

Coming to his own, Rastín knew he dared not speak, so he looked on silently, unable to keep hatred from his eyes.

"We disgust you. We abhor you…and yet you amuse us," the king said. Speaking to someone Rastín could not see, the king asked, "Pray, do tell us of little king's last."

A serpent magi slithered across the floor. Its head had two great horns, its long muscular torso rested on a serpent's body, and its body otherwise covered in gold and black scales had a broad strip of reddish scales running from its chest down the front of its body. "The little king told us, 'The Túrring crown shall be passed to my son, my heir. House Túrring shall stand and our people shall serve your masters as one.' "

Still holding Rastín by the back of his shirt, the king asked, "And did the duplicitous ones serve us as one?"

"No, no, your majesty, they did not."

"And yet we keep the little king's own—and have we mistreated it?"

"No, no, your majesty, we have not."

"Indeed, we have not. Perhaps this little bit of nothing would like to be impaled upon the roasting spit and served up with the others of his kind?"

Revulsion getting the better of common sense, Rastín stared directly at the king.

"Sullen, angry, little plaything. Does it want to say something?" Before Rastín had even started to speak, the king began shaking him and repeated his question. "Does it want to say something?"

As Rastín started to speak, the king tossed him up into the air, and now Rastín knew for certain that the great hall had a ceiling. He would have crashed into it had the king not snatched him out of the air an instant before impact.

"Plaything," the king said, "be careful lest you cease to amuse us."

"I am Rastín Dnyarr Túrring, of House Túrring. I am my father's heir. My people are the Élvemere and we have never done harm to your people."

When Rastín spoke, every other sound in the great hall fell away. The king kept his awed followers in check with a glance while he gripped Rastín between two fingers like a doll. "And yet you have done harm this very moment, by your very words. House Túrring, indeed. I do recall the little king standing before me. And did he not then cower and beg on his knees?"

The serpent magi said, "The little king begged and groveled on his knees. He begged your majesty to spare his people and the life of his son."

"My father could not have knelt before anyone," Rastín said boldly. "His body was ravaged from the waist down."

Without warning, the king dropped Rastín. The fall from over half a chain would have seriously injured the untrained, but Rastín rolled as he landed, distributing the impact. As he started to stand, Dierá grabbed his right arm in both of her hands and pulled him to his knees beside her.

The king's raucous laughter returned. "And did the little king not tell you it was he who declared war on us? We merely asked for homage and tribute. And did we not spare his people and his heir in the end?"

"Your majesty did most graciously, and for very little, I might add. One royal person to spare the people. One-half royal person to spare the son."

"One and one-half royal persons indeed, and what grand entertainment. The little king plotting and scheming. The little queen going behind his back. The little king pleading and begging for the little queen. The little queen with more pleading and begging until I finally delighted of her flesh."

"You spin lies within lies!" Rastín shouted. "My mother died in the camps. My father's legs were gone of the wasting before we came to this accursed place."

Without word or warning, the king snatched Rastín up from the ground, took up the spear of a guard and impaled Rastín. Dierá's screams and cries for mercy were nothing compared to the death rattle from Rastín's lungs as the spear entered his body between his legs and exploded out of his chest.

CHAPTER TEN

Dierá was inconsolable when she returned to the cell. Whether she opened or closed her eyes, she saw only Rastín impaled, and it drove her to hysterics and madness. She was a shieldmaiden of the Élvemere, and yet she had done nothing but whimper and cower before the great king. She had failed her people utterly; she had failed her king utterly.

It was a day before she could lift her head and do anything other than sob. A day more before G'rkyr and the other Empyrjurin got her to speak. Her first coherent words were a prayer to the Mother, begging for forgiveness and strength. She needed the Mother's forgiveness to face herself. She needed strength to keep herself from slipping back into tears. Then just when she thought her heart could not break any further, she thought of Eldri and Síari, the sisters of her heart if not of her blood. Eldri was lost to her now and Síari had taken the Long Road.

G'rkyr and Zanük cared for Dierá as they would have one of their own, and their fondness for the elf maiden grew. By the evening of the third day, G'rkyr could not contain himself, but it was Zanük who spoke for his brother. "Dierá," he pleaded, "For G'rkyr's sake, you must eat and you must return to yourself. We Empyrjurin do not often find what G'rkyr thinks he's found with you."

Dierá lifted her head, regarded Zanük with eyes full of tears. Normally she found G'rkyr's infatuation with her endearing, but at this moment she could only think of the impossibility of relations with an Empyrjurin. It was absurd. It was beyond absurd. Before she could stop herself, the anger and bitterness behind her tears became words. "I am Élvemere," she shouted. "He is Empyrjurin. Our people cannot mix. It is absurd. We are all pets of the masters. Would you have me as a pet too? Would I then be the pet of a pet?"

Zanük's response surprised Dierá. Turning to his brother, he said, "Tell her."

"I cannot," G'rkyr responded. "His Empirical Majestic Exalted One brought this on himself."

"Tell her or I will tell her."

Something in G'rkyr's expression stirred Dierá and helped her focus. "Tell me what? What can you not tell me?"

G'rkyr said nothing. Zanük spoke instead. "Was he truly a prince, a prince of the Élvemere?"

"More than a prince," Dierá said, "He was the son of the High King. When the king passed on to the blessed land, he became heir apparent. Save for the crowning, he was the High King of Élvemere. In my heart he remains my king."

At the same time G'rkyr said, "His Exaltedness was a king?" Zanük said, "I see now. What were you to him?"

Dierá started to speak, but held her tongue. She had already said too much.

"Very well," Zanük said, "but you must know G'rkyr is more than just G'rkyr?"

Dierá furrowed her brow, her eyes revealing a question she wanted to ask but did not. As her face paled and her expression fell away, Zanük raised the bowl of stewed meat and helped her eat. Nothing was said for a time, and then for some small amount of time Dierá slept.

When she awoke, one of the young female gargants was beside her and neither Zanük nor G'rkyr were to be found. Dierá asked of them in both the language of the Élvemere and the language of the Empyrjurin, but the other would not speak.

She was beside herself with tears by the time the brothers returned. When she saw them dressed in finery as if they had just returned from a celebration, she sobbed. Of the two, only Zanük approached her. G'rkyr seemed to want nothing to do with her.

When Zanük crouched beside her, Dierá lashed out at him. "Do you celebrate the death of my king with the masters? Do you gloat in my sorrow? Did you feast and drink to our deaths?"

Zanük reached out to her, putting his left hand on her shoulder, but it enveloped much of her small figure, too. "We do not celebrate death. We do not gloat. We do not feast and drink. We are as you."

"You are not as me! I have never been given another as a gift!"

"You are more punishment than gift," G'rkyr said quietly.

"What does he mean by that?" Dierá demanded.

"He means the masters' gifts are cruel as this day was cruel."

"Cruel?" Dierá shouted. "How can celebration be cruel?"

As she said it, she knew she should not have, because Zanük pulled away from her as she did so; and none of the Empyrjurin spoke to her for the rest of the day. She pretended to be hurt by his actions, when in truth she was more confused. She did not eat her evening meal. She cast her food and drink on the floor.

When none of this roused their sympathy, she pretended to be sick and faint. When this got no response, she went to the open cistern on the other side of the room and disrobed, slipping into the cool waters. Scrubbing herself clean occupied her for a time. As she started to relax and drift away, she forgot she was trying to draw G'rkyr's attention and simply enjoyed one of the few pleasures that remained to her.

As she drifted there in the cool waters, her father's face floated before her eyes. In this dreamlike state, she spoke with him as if he was there before her. "I have twice failed, father," she said. "He did not see me as his queen, his equal. He did not love me even as I loved him. As I stood before the ageless, I could do nothing save tremble and watch him stumble onward to his death."

Her father took her hand in his. "Athania Dierá Steorra, you could not have changed the course once set upon."

"But I have the gift, father. I could have turned this aside, if only I had chosen to do so."

"To reveal such a thing…to what end…to your ruin?"

"We dwell within the mists of ruin. Our age is a lost age, as our people are a lost people. I chose inaction when action was called for and—"

"—and you chose selflessly. You put the needs of our people above the needs of your heart. You became a queen, when a queen was most needed. A queen cannot always follow her heart, and you have learned this, though the cost has been dear, very dear. But I sense that… I sense—"

Her father's words cut off and she could see him no more. The transition was so abrupt that she sank into the waters of the cistern and came up sputtering, gasping for air. As she started to go under again, G'rkyr scooped her out of the water and put her on the ground beside the cistern, where she choked and wheezed as she struggled to take in a breath while coughing up water she had swallowed.

After she finally took in several deep breaths, she threw her arms around G'rkyr's midsection. "I'm sorry," she told the gargant. "I didn't mean to lash out at you."

Uncomfortable with her nakedness against him, G'rkyr handed Dierá her slip and then turned away as he waited for her to put it on. "You meant it, Dierá," G'rkyr said with his back turned to her. "You meant every word because you do not understand. The masters are as cruel to us as they are to you. In Jurin, today is Atonement's last day. Atonement is our celebration of the cycle's end and the coming of the time when day and night are the same.

"The masters...made Zanük and I...dress up and attend their feast...to my people's fall...on our most...sacred of days. Your face...in my thoughts...is what..."

Dierá hushed him by thrusting herself against his side. "I'm sorry, G'rkyr. I thought only of myself, of my loss. The ageless king is most cruel."

G'rkyr held her small form as she clung to him. "The fat one who lords over us is not a king. He acts the part of one, but he is not a king. You and I are not important enough to be taken before the master's king, though perhaps Rastín was if what you said of him was true."

Dierá moved around to stand in front of G'rkyr so she could look up at his face. "Not a king, but he said he was a king."

"He may have been called by royal title, but he would never dare to name himself a king. He is but a slavelord, one of a hundred hundred such among the masters. This world is his bounds, no doubt for displeasing the masters' king, and so he turns his displeasure to our suffering."

"You know the masters well. Zanük said that you were more. What did he mean by that?"

G'rkyr withdrew from Dierá for a moment, started to say something, but then became quiet. Zanük spoke for his brother. "We, of course, know the masters well, for we have only just fallen."

"Fallen?"

G'rkyr said, "He means to say we were once masters, not true equals to the drakónus or the titanus, but masters the same. Now, we are fallen. We are as you."

Dierá could not believe what she was hearing. "And you, G'rkyr, are more?"

"I am," the gargant admitted. "My father is Nük T'nyr. King of the Empyrjurin."

"And Zanük?"

"Zanük is Zanük."

"Why was I given to you?"

"A cruel joke, a twisting, a glimmer of what once we had. Now that we've taken to you it is certain—"

"You speak of drakónus and titanus."

"The slavelord is Drakón. Dragon in your language, I believe. Most of his sworn are S'h'dith, the snake people. The watcher, he is titanus. Titans as you know them."

Dierá reached out to G'rkyr. "But you said you were at war with the masters?"

"And we are," said Zanük.

G'rkyr added, "We are, Dierá, and I must tell you—"

"Brother," interrupted Zanük, "She does not need to hear you say what she already suspects. I will say it for you and spare you anguish." Zanük paused, taking in Dierá's expression. "The answer to the unspoken is yes. We are a warrior people known for our ferocity. We are savage, brutal, and without fear in battle. I am bred to this, as is G'rkyr, as are all Empyrjurin. An age ago, the masters rewarded our people for countless battles won across countless worlds by raising us up. My father sought to reach too far…This is our cost…"

Dierá balled up her hands into fists. "But you are not savage. You are not brutal. You are not cruel."

"We are more so," G'rkyr said quietly. "We are Empyrjurin. These things are our life—"

Zanük spoke heatedly with G'rkyr in a language Dierá did not know. These words brought the other Empyrjurin from the recesses of the cell. Five larger females spoke with Zanük and G'rkyr in this same language, then one Dierá did not recognize came forth. After this one spoke, all became quiet.

Zanük broke the silence. Speaking in the language of the Jurin peoples, he said, "My mother wishes to know of you."

"Your mother?" Dierá replied in the same language.

The one never before seen gazed at Dierá, and Dierá saw what she had not seen before. The five larger females were older; the one was fully grown. As understanding came, she bowed her head and knelt before the queen of the Empyrjurin.

Zanük repeated his statement, adding, "A rare trust she grants you."

Dierá stood, unconsciously fixing her slip and smoothing back her hair. She hesitated before to tell the Empyrjurins who she was, but she did not hesitate now. She said clearly and carefully in the Jurin language, "I am Athania Dierá Steorra, a shieldmaiden of the Élvemere. In Élvemere, I was to have been a queen, a wife to Rastín Dnyarr Túrring, son of the High King of Élvemere."

Realizing something unsaid, Dierá turned to Zanük, but the gargant recognized the question in Dierá's eyes even before she asked it. "You want to know the obvious, to know why G'rkyr and I are not important enough if my mother is what you suspect."

Dierá nodded, finding a new softness to his brutish face.

"My mother has right of birth over Three Hammers clanfolk. The other clans have their great mothers. Our people have but one great father. King Nük T'nyr, my father."

As Zanük spoke, Dierá regarded G'rkyr and the queen. "In Élvemere, the kingdoms of my people each have their kings and queens. My father, Alborn Steorra, was king of Dobehen."

Zanük's expression became stern, the equivalent of a smile. "You, Dierá, are more as G'rkyr is more. You are a daughter of a king, and yet—"

"Dobehen was the first kingdom to fall to the ageless. My people speak of it only as a curse. To say that you come from this place where the ruin of the Élvemere began is to say you are nothing, so what I tell you is that I am nothing."

"You speak an untruth to play against what my people value most. It does not change my opinion of you. Your line is one of strength. My father led the ageless to glory countless times and he struck the strongest first. Break resolve by breaking strength. It is the way."

Dierá blew out a long breath and looked up at Zanük. "Truly?"

"It is as it is."

The Empyrjurins began speaking in the language Dierá did not understand. The queen spoke at length. G'rkyr and Zanük made several responses, but mostly listened. When the queen finished speaking, there was a sudden uproar among the Empyrjurins. G'rkyr and Zanük beat back one of the large females just before the queen retreated to the dark recesses of the cavernous cell.

When G'rkyr and Zanük returned, Dierá put her hands on her hips and glared at them. She wanted to know what happened, and she hoped her stance showed the strength the gargants so highly respected.

G'rkyr's response was laughter that boomed and echoed throughout the cell. To Dierá, it seemed laughter was the one thing all peoples shared, but she suspected that gargant's laughter was a show of scorn rather than humor.

Zanük said, "G'rkyr leave us." G'rkyr stopped laughing, his expression hardened, but he left without comment, leaving Dierá alone with Zanük. "He seeks to show my mother his heart remains hardened with fire. He will not be himself until he has proven this to her."

"And why must his heart be hardened with fire?"

Zanük's laughter followed the echoes of his brother's. "G'rkyr has refused to take the thing he wants—and that thing is you. But that is as nothing to what my mother wishes."

"Go on," Dierá said as she cast a sidelong glance to G'rkyr who lurked just at the edge of the shadows.

"Before I continue, I must know the truth of you."

Dierá turned back to Zanük and gave the gargant her full attention. "I'm listening."

"In your own words, you told us you knew nothing of the Jurin peoples save what you've learned in books and had been told. Those things you read and learned—"

"—were in preparation for this day, this moment. The moment when the sons of the Empyrjurin king chose an elf maiden over their own people—and you have chosen, have you not?"

Zanük's face burned with the living fire of his people. "How could you possibly know such a thing?"

"It was what I was born to," Dierá said, almost bitterly. "Tell me now of the dream, the wish, the desire of my heart and make it truth."

"But you—do you—" His words shifted to the language Dierá did not understand. When she did not react, he returned to Jurin language. "—you do not—and yet—"

"I have not the true gift, only a part of the gift. My mother had the gift and she saw my futures—the turnings of the many paths, spreading ever outward like the branches of the Eternal Tree." She paused, closed her eyes, sucked in a long breath. "Please," she begged, "this not knowing is torture beyond imagining."

Zanük said, "Karthar would never kill such a king or even the son of such king with his own hand. Rastín must be among the twice-born now. If so, he is forever lost to us, for he exists in living death and now knows only the service of the masters."

Dierá said nothing in reply, thinking to herself only of how little the Empyrjurin knew of the Élvemere.

CHAPTER ELEVEN

What Rastín perceived and what actually happened could not have been the same thing. Instead of joyful arrival in the blessed land, he found himself in a gray room with walls so close he felt he could not turn around. The sole furnishings in the gray room were a bed of straw, a wooden bucket, and a door.

It seemed as if life before this room was but a dream, yet memories of flat, open fields did not fade. When he closed his eyes, he walked with his mother among great oaks, rigid pines, and willful elms. Together, they sang to the ancient ones to coax them from their deep slumber. The ancient ones preferred songs in the languages of the first peoples, so Rastín and his mother sang their songs using the words of those long lost.

Upon waking, the oldest of the ancients spoke of nothing save root and bark, earth and water, wind and leaves. It took concerted effort to get them to lift their roots from the earth and speak of other things. When they finally did speak, they did so in the language of nature. A purposeful blending of the sounds of babbling brook, rustling leaves, and gushing wind was an act of welcoming, cordial and sincere. Rastín did his best to weave and thread the wild magics required to respond in kind, but in truth he did not enjoy the long talk with all its formalities and requisites.

Fortunately, the young ones among the ancients did not care for all the formalities and requisites of the long talk. They would uproot and take Rastín to far off places where the elders would not walk. Places where the Fhur peoples dwelled, and where he learned the customs of the Fhurjurin, Fhurtrollen, and Fhurgnomen. Places where the Spiraren peoples dwelled, and where he learned about the places between places. Even lost places where Entspiraren still dwelled, although the ancients and Spiraren had gone their separate ways ages ago.

Often the young ancients would play games with him. His favorite was one where they spoke on behalf of the forest, and he had to guess for whom they spoke. Even now he evoked flashes of sunlight, wind blowing across gray-green leaves, and glimpses of small purple flowers. He knew this plant well—it was sage—and so he raced off in search of it.

When Rastín spotted a thick patch of the plentiful shrub, he knelt down beside it to take in its musty yet smoky aroma. As he stood and turned to seek permission to pick some for his mother, he saw a pair of eyes glowing behind a tangled mass of branches. The glowing eyes startled him, but as looked closer he saw that what he mistook for branches were thick locks of hair, twisted and tied.

He stepped toward the mud-covered creature, not sure why he was not afraid. Perhaps it was because the young ancients had not called out in alarm, as they would have done if he were in danger. If he had been closer to the great river, he might have mistaken the creature for one of the S'h'dith, the snake people, but this beastlike creature was not S'h'dith.

A word, a name, came to him. *Wërg.* As he watched the creature, he knew it was telling him this, though it used no words to do so. Another word came to him. *Akharran.* And he knew that was the creature's name.

Suddenly, he felt as if he was in one of the places between places. It was bitter cold, dark, and lonely, yet he was not alone. The one called Akharran was there with him. She was somehow recognizable. She was transformed into a being of subtle beauty, no longer a mud-covered beast. Only her eyes were unchanged.

In this form, she could have passed for Élvemere, yet her skin was bronzed; her hair, long and dark; and her figure, full. She was at least a hand and a span taller than him as well.

"Here we reconcile," she said in the language of Rastín's people. "It was your father's final behest."

"I've only just left my father," Rastín said. "He rides for S'amore in Dobehen to speak to King Alborn."

"He will arrive too late and with too few to push back the Empyrjurin. Dobehen falls, and Élvemere within a fortnight."

Rastín forced himself to remain calm. "You speak false."

Akharran took his hand in hers and her touch felt familiar even as she said, "Dny, we don't have much time. You must listen. You must remember. In this place, you can become one with both your selves."

"I don't understand. What is happening? What is this place?"

"Your father and mother…They knew, they saw. They showed me. Dny, if I can save you, I can save my people. Already your children in my womb give me your words, and you give me your ways. One day my people will rise anew and retake what is ours. As perhaps one day you will retake what is yours."

"The Wërg?"

"Yes, Wërg," she told him. "But on the day we retake what is ours, we will no longer be Wërg. We will be Wërmere, and you will know us by this name just as you will know the children of these as Wolmerrelle."

Suddenly, unexpectedly, he saw the gray room looming before his eyes. He called out to Akharran, tried to hold on to her, tried to remain in the place between places. Akharran called out, "You are Rastín Dnyarr Túrring, son of the High King of Élvemere. Know this and remember."

Bright light from the open door hurt, his eyes watered as he squinted and blinked. Chained and manacled slaves of a winged and horned race entered and took Rastín away.

Rastín was dragged along dark pathways, and then suddenly he was in great round room. The room's vaulted ceiling was covered in a mural and its walls were hung with rich tapestries. The mural depicted twin yellow suns in a cloudy sky. The tapestries, meticulously drawn battle scenes.

Before a dais, he was pushed to the floor. He remained this way for some time, even as he heard those who had brought him withdraw. When he dared risk it, he raised his head to see another stalking along the edge of the dais. Although he could only see it from ankle to shin, it was enough for him to know that this one was more like him than unlike him, even if very large.

"You may rise," the other said in a deep, thunderous voice.

Unsure whether to stand or kneel before this one, Rastín stopped part way between. With his head respectfully downcast, he tried to remember things before the gray room. As if from another's dream, he saw places, things, and peoples he knew he had never seen, but they were oddly familiar. A voice was speaking to him, but the words were in an unknown language. Horror enveloped him as he realized the images he saw were from the tapestries, and yet the things he saw he knew.

The one on the dais struck him, the other's hand enveloping his head. Still reeling as he stumbled sideways, Rastín looked up at the whole of the towering figure. As he watched the other speak, the meaning of the words spoken came to him in spite of the other's thick unknown accent.

"Starved and delirious," the other called out. "You've made him useless! Remove him."

The chained and manacled slaves returned. Rastín heard and felt them grip his arms, but he did not see them. He saw only the images flashing before his eyes—the tapestry images. And then he realized what he should have known from the first. He heard the words spoken previously and became Rastín Dnyarr Túrring, son of the High King of Élvemere.

He stood, throwing off the hands of the slaves. "You are Ky'el, son of Rnothen, of the titans," he said.

With a wave of his hand, the titan sent the slaves running from the room. "Tell me, scrawny one. Tell me of the theatrics on the calends of Atonement. Did you truly sacrifice yourself for me as Karthar claims?"

"S'amore was razed when my father arrived, riding at the head of the armies of the Élvemere. You glory in this, the battles my people lost."

"The memories are yours, Túrring. You rode at your father's side, I know not how. Now tell me, does Karthar speak truth?"

Hearing the name a second time brought a flood of memories he somehow shared with the ageless slavelord. "I did not ride with my father to Dobehen's aid. I was not—"

"The tapestries do not lie, Túrring. They show what I wish to see, and what I wish to see is your worthiness to be called to my service among the twice-born. It is a rare one who has memories of things beyond the gray room. Usually it takes many tendays, a cycle sometimes, of conditioning to regain a shadow of one's past self. And yet—"

"I stand before you, no shadow of my past self."

"Indeed, so it would appear." Ky'el seemed pleased by Rastín's forwardness, if only fleetingly so. "Or perhaps you are more clever than most." Ky'el sat in a large, plush chair. He studied Rastín as Rastín studied him. Just as a voice from a distant place called out the reckoning toll, Ky'el said, "Kneel before me and beg to be among the twice-born."

"I will never kneel before you or anyone again," Rastín said boldly. As Ky'el stood, his eyes seemingly probing for Rastín's inner thoughts, Rastín was overwhelmed by the irrational feeling that what was occurring was never seen before.

"Though ignobility suits you well enough, you will. You will kneel before me; you will kneel before all. You will not do so out of esteem or reverence, but because you must."

Rastín dropped to his knees, but did not bow his head. At this, Ky'el bared his teeth in a broad, angry smile.

"And so Karthar…Was it his intention to have me take you to service, or to have me doubt and cast you back? Clever…clever…The son of a high king, no less. The power of the line mine if I but dare…"

Throwing his arms back, hands with fingers outstretched, eyes wide, Ky'el called out in the language of the ageless. The tapestries spun their tales. The ceiling mural flowed. Time passed. Rastín remained where he was, kneeling, looking up at the titan.

Then without word or warning, the titan turned on Rastín, unleashing his full fury. Rastín instinctively dodged the blows with the lithe precision that set the Élvemere apart from most other peoples.

"It was you," Ky'el said as he lashed out at Rastín. "You wanted death, invited it, and took it in—did not find it. Yet I know not whether to applaud or jeer. Death to you is not solace as sweet as retribution, and I offer you a chance at such as you only dared to hope for."

Rastín countered the titan's fists with a series of feints, never daring to strike back. His increasingly feral eyes showed the beast within him trying to break loose even as Ky'el took up a long metal rod and struck out with blow after blow.

Ky'el's eyes never left Rastín's. "I give you permission to strike back. Show me what you are capable of, land blows on my person, and you'll never again need permission to strike out at one who has set upon you. I know you want this! Take it!"

Rastín obeyed. Ky'el's rod became a ceaselessly moving blur. Rastín fought on. To break through the wall of air and metal, he used quick jabs and sharp thrusts with both hands and feet. Pain was his only reward.

"Half starved and you fight with resolve and single-minded fury that is almost admirable. Too bad you'll rot in this place and wonder to the end of your last miserable day what could have been."

Undaunted, Rastín pushed on, unleashing the beast within him. A lifetime's worth of wrath and rage poured out of him. His hands and fists became moving blurs, matching the moving blur that was the rod expertly wielded by Ky'el.

One moment his feet were striking out, the next his hands. The dais became his springboard. He used it to reach heights on a par with the titan. Turning, twisting, launching, tumbling—ever moving.

The rod in Ky'el's hand halted mid-blow. Rastín pulled back even as Ky'el recovered.

"Kneel," Ky'el commanded. "Accept judgment. Swift death or life in service—both better than rotting in this place."

Rastín dropped to one knee, bowed his head, and waited.

"I find you undeserving. You failed to touch my person. How would you ever battle Empyrjurin clanlords, shadowriders, or even the eternal—?"

Without looking up, Rastín launched forward, tumbled, spun in the air and struck out with a high kick, his foot catching the titan under the chin. He landed on both feet and hands like an animal, head raised, eyes watching. Poised, ready to launch again, he waited.

"Indeed," Ky'el said. Rastín waited, unsure whether the titan was pleased or displeased, although the other's air of peerless superiority returned. Ky'el called out to those unseen, "Remove him."

Two chained ones entered. Rastín's expression clouded. "I'll not return willingly."

"I expected no less." The titan focused, reached out with his right hand, and drew a line in the air. The manacles and chains the guards wore dropped away. "These two failed as you failed, and yet I asked Karthar to withhold punishment and retain them. I'll offer no such quittance to you. You have not earned it."

Rastín said nothing. He eyed the two as they picked up their weighted chains and wielded them before him. He held firm, watching the rhythmic movement of the chains. It seemed he had to focus to see them and the chains. As they hurled the weighted ends of the chains at him, he tumbled backward and spun to the right, where he picked up the titan's metal rod.

Normally such a heavy weapon would be ineffective in the hands of one as lean and slight of frame as he, yet he had worked the dark land as both elves and beasts did. He bore the long rod before him as few could, lashing out left and right, striking first one and then the other.

Recovering, the two took to the air, their powerful wings making them agile, fast, and sprightly. It was two against one, but Rastín held his own. As they circled and attacked, Rastín defended, the long rod giving him advantage over the long chains even as their wings gave them advantage over his feet.

Nevertheless, the two were beating Rastín back. With the wall looming a double step behind, he hefted the rod, focused, and then hurled the rod like a javelin in a desperate gambit. He caught one of the two full in the chest. As the one crashed to the floor, unmoving and lifeless, the other caught him with the chain, ripping his legs out from under him.

Rastín tumbled to the floor, the whole of his left side taking the full force of the impact. He spun and pulled to rid himself of the chain, only to bring the other closer. He swung up with his right arm, catching its leg near the thigh.

The other pumped its powerful wings, and Rastín thrust out with his shoulder, throwing the full force of his weight and strength into the other's lower abdomen. His battering ram approach felled the other. In an instant Rastín was sitting on the other's chest, gripping the other's head between his hands and bashing its head against the raised edge of the dais.

"Enough," Ky'el called out.

Rastín looked up, straightened. Ky'el focused, reached out with his right hand and drew a mark in the air. A knowing expression on the titan's face spoke to Rastín. Rastín looked down; found he was standing over an Empyrjurin. He looked over to the other, finding one of his own people where once the winged and horned one had lain.

He staggered over to his fallen brethren still impaled on the rod. As he leaned down to remove the rod, his brows knotted with anguish. He glared at the titan, even as he sank to his knees.

CHAPTER TWELVE

Twice-born. It was a curse. Rastín was as sure of this now as anything. Rocking on his knees, hot tears rolled down his cheeks. He flung his head back and cried out, "What have I done?"

Ky'el focused his eyes on the fallen, swept his hand in a wide arc. They vanished, only their discarded chains and manacles remaining. "What you have done is convince me of your worthiness. Now put on their chains and manacles."

Rastín glowered at the titan. "I will not put on another's chains."

Ky'el stepped from the dais, pointed, and gripped Rastín without reaching out. Although Rastín struggled, he could not break free of the invisible hands. "Very well, it is decided then."

"It is," Rastín said through clenched teeth.

"Your training was adequate and no doubt the best you could gain under such conditions, but it has not fully prepared you. You have enough knowledge of the Path to strike those who walk in and out of it at will as those two could, and yet you do not know enough to understand or walk the Path yourself. You would last a few battles, perhaps, but not—"

"Try me."

"In my service, you will ever deal in death. Should I command it, you will fight to your last breath. You won't negotiate. You won't capitulate. You will do. You will act. You will die."

Rastín gave no sign of agreement. Ky'el pointed to the ceiling. He began to rise and Rastín, still gripped by the invisible hand, rose with him. When it seemed they must crash into the top of the dome, they emerged into a vast open space where twin yellow suns shone down from a cloudy sky, and far below great pillars stood among ruins.

Ky'el landed amid the ruins. "Tivarus, the world of my birth," he said as he released Rastín.

Nearby, the wellspring of a stream flowed into the air, where it joined other streams and became a leagues-long river that floated in the air and flowed to the floating mountains in the distance. A myriad of creatures swam within and about the waters of the river— glass snakes, terrapins, fish.

A colossal fish, with a large forked tail and pointed head, pitched out of the river. An enormous glass snake followed. Rastín lost sight of both as one of the great terrapins settled to the ground and blotted out the view.

The terrapin was so massive and old that the whiskers around its mouth were as thick as tree trunks. Ky'el scaled one of the flippers, climbing onto the terrapin's thick shell. Rastín followed. On top of the shell was a long, enclosed shelter with many windows and doors; racing toward them from the closest door were many stout warriors with pallid skin, black hair, and orange eyes.

The warriors carried war axes and battle hammers, and following was a green-skinned gargant with a thick green beard, webbed feet, and webbed hands. The gargant and the titan embraced as friends, with Ky'el picking up the gargant and then the gargant picking up Ky'el.

The crack of whips and searing pain gave Rastín a stark reality check. He sank to his knees, putting his arms with hands in fists behind his head to protect his face, ears, and neck.

In the language of the iron peoples, Ky'el told the others, "Put him in the pits or the dregs. Feed him to the Drakón for all I care. But make sure he knows death and hate when his time comes." To Rastín, he said in the language of the Élvemere, "One day you will thank me for this, but that day is a long way off."

Then Rastín was dragged into the bowels of what he would later know as a ship—one that went wherever the terrapin went, whether across or beneath water. Beyond thick iron bars of his dark cell, he saw a torch in a sconce fixed to the wall. Its dirty orange flame flickered in a draft he could not see. He thought it meant the terrapin was moving.

Days passed. Rastín lived in the murky cell much as he had lived in the gray room. Thoughts about things beyond the cell began to seem like a dream. He thought of the words in the language of the iron peoples that Ky'el had spoken, and the voices he heard faintly now in this same language. He was sure the stout ones were Fedwëorgs—iron dwarves—and the one who had greeted Ky'el was a sæjurin—a sea gargant. But what were Fedwëorgs doing with sæjurins? And for that matter, why were they helping Ky'el—a titan?

Realizing these thoughts were no longer his own, he rocked back and forth. With his face in his hands, he shivered and told himself, "I am Rastín Dnyarr Túrring, son of the High King of Élvemere."

But the voices in his head would not let him be Rastín Dnyarr Túrring, son of the High King of Élvemere. One voice told him that he was twice-born and that he had no past. Another told him that the days of the Élvemere had long since passed; and if there ever were such a people, he was surely the last one. Yet another told him he must now awaken and find the Wërg within him.

While he listened to the voices, it was the last voice that roused him from his dreams. "You are awake," the voice said.

Rastín looked up at the unfamiliar face. "Where am I?"

"If there is a Hellplace, this surely is it—and this you well know."

Rastín stood, looked down at a thick waist and thigh that he did not recognize, though it was his own. "Who are you? What has happened?"

The dark-haired man with the hazel eyes said, "I am Martin of Voethe—you know this, Yarr."

"Yarr?"

"You," Martin said, stabbing a finger into Rastín's chest. "You've taken one too many beatings in the pit. I didn't think you were going to come back after that last one, but—"

"The language you speak?"

"That of the Kingdoms of Men—you know this. You are the only one I can speak to in this accursed place. You learned my words and I many of yours. You spoke for me when I could not."

Rastín wheeled around, glared at the iron gates, and turned back. "How long here?"

"You mean, for you?" Martin did not wait for a response. He pulled Rastín to a corner of the cell where hundreds of marks were etched into the wall. "These are your marks—you tell me how long."

He ran a hand over the marks. "And this pit?"

Martin pushed Rastín to a crude, wooden table. "I've saved your rations for the last three days. Eat, regain your strength. There would be more but at the first I was unsure…Your wounds were grave."

He sat, ate, hung his head. After a long while, Rastín looked up to find Martin nearby. "I thank you for what you've done for me. I will repay what—"

"You've already repaid me many times previous. I only regret that I have no skill in the ways as you. If I had, I could have healed your wounds as you've healed mine."

Rastín's eyes tightened. "I've…healed you?"

"You've taught me the ways of will and dream and spirit, though I have no skill at such. All I can do is put to mind what you teach me and hope to pass it on to others."

"How long have you been in this place with me?"

"Since the snows of the last cycle and the snows come again."

Rastín reached for the jug. Somehow he misjudged, and the next thing he knew water was spilling across the table. Martin righted the jug, pouring what little was left into a clay mug.

Rastín drank, sat back. His eyes became weights he could no longer lift.

"Come on, Yarr," Martin said.

Rastín nodded, stood with Martin's help. Martin led him to the other side of the cell, where a rustic bed waited. He sat heavily. Martin stood over him for a moment, his bearded, mannish face somehow comforting.

"This new one you speak of in your sleep. This Dierá. You loved her, yes?"

Rastín found pain and emptiness, but no answers.

"No need to answer. I see it. Now I know why you fight like Great Father himself is at your side. But why do you think of her now after all this time?"

Rastín eyes closed of their own accord. He was done. His arms and legs had gone numb and he could no longer feel any pain. It felt as if he were falling away, as if everything around him was gone and no more. He felt himself settle upon a surface as firm and cold as an altar stone.

Fingers brushed through his hair and down the side of his face, and though they had no true substance, he knew the touch.

"Dierá," he said, and found it strange that he could speak while the rest of his body was numb.

"You have forgotten me," a voice said. It was her voice, but distant somehow though she spoke right in his ear.

"I have not," he said, "I've forgotten myself, but I've not forgotten you."

"Oh, but you have," the voice said. "You call me with her name and yet you know I am not her."

He wanted to grab her hand and pull her to him, but he could not move. He tried to open his eyes.

"Do not," she said. "You will not find the one you look for. I am not her."

Even as he sought to ask who she was, he knew. "Akharran?"

"Yes, my love. Be calm. I've much to tell you and little time before we must both return to the waking world."

PART II
CYVAIR

The Cycle 11231
Drakón Standard

Kurhri da'm te nurrin var ma'hdden

Kurhri adda'tten te garran var sa'dron

Kurhri mo'rren te hurre var de'trod

To blessed victory above all else

To blessed allegiance beyond measure

To blessed death without regret
—From the *Empyrjurin Credo*

CHAPTER THIRTEEN

Battles raged across the hundred worlds. The empire burned. King Nük T'nyr turned his sights on the seats of power. "Kurhri da'm te nurrin var ma'hdden," he shouted as he led his armies down from the mountains under the cover of darkness.

"Kurhren da'mer se nurrem var ma'hddri," his soldiers shouted out in reply.

Ten leagues distant from the walls of the eternal city the fight began. His armies clashed with the vanguard of the Drakón defenders. "Estygin ma'hn var der'x gher," he commanded. His commanders relayed the order. His armies dug in.

By the time pre-dawn twilight began to reveal the landscape, trenches extended back to the mountains and stretched in every direction across the valley as far as the eye could see—every direction except ahead, because in that direction lay the great city with its ten leagues of rank-and-file defenders.

The dance of war was constant. Thousand-member lines of defenders marched on his trenches; the armies clashed. His soldiers poured out of the trenches; the armies clashed. Through it all, Nük T'nyr's soldiers greeted the defenders with laughter—laughter that boomed and echoed to the mountains and through the valley to show their scorn as they fought the slave armies of a hundred enslaved worlds.

As the sky cracked and lightning fell through, Nük T'nyr turned his eyes to the heavens and cried out, "Kurhri da'm te trerrin sur umdeh'n," and his armies prepared for death to rain down upon them. Death came in the form of the Drakón—a thousand score Drakón, breathing so much fire and death that the air tasted of brimstone, smoke, and copper, and the trenches ran with blood.

The survivors—and there were many tens of thousands—rose up, riding waves of will and force and attacking with the full ferocity of the Jurin peoples. Fhurjurin retaliated with earth and rock. Empyrjurin purged the skies with living flame. Styrjurin raged with lightning and storm. Monsjurin and Hylljurin turned their war machines away from the lines and to the skies.

The defenders surged ahead, moving into the forward trenches. Time slowed, as it often did for Nük T'nyr in battle. He could feel the sacred eum flow to his blade, feeding the living flames, as he cut a wide swath through a line of defenders. At his side, his hand-selected Slaedwa, clad in crimson, fought.

He called out in tribute to a fallen comrade, "Kurhri se mo'rren sur Ghul Rwern." His voice roared above the din of war. For many long beats, it seemed the fallen general fought beside him, lending strength to his cause and blade. He did not mourn Ghul Rwern. Empyrjurin did not mourn righteous passing. They celebrated it in word and deed.

Cutting his way through a line of scaly Gnogish pikers, he found himself facing lines of goblin charioteers and dragon soldiers. The goblin charioteers were accompanied by packs of dogs. The soldiers riding the wingless dragons wore thick plated mail, wielded great double-bladed swords, and defended with triangular shields with long curved spikes on each corner and on the faces of the shields. The dragons, a smaller, witless race of their distant cousins, raced on two legs, attacking with their shorter forelegs while breathing fey fire.

Kha'el D'erth hadn't yet noticed these new adversaries, for the general was commanding the catapult squads and focused on the far lines and the skies, but Praefect L'kohn was facing the oncoming forces. His face was slowly transforming from annoyance to fury, for the targets of the goblin charioteers and dragon soldiers were the machines of war, not the Jurin lines or the Scarabaeid. Their attacks, at right angles to the catapults and ballistae, in preparation for the strike known as the pincer, aimed at breaking the Jurin defenses and making wreckage of their wooden support platforms.

In a long, slow moment of calculation, Nük T'nyr considered the possibilities. Praefect L'kohn and his Scarabaeid could not turn their focus away from feeding and guiding the machines of war. If they did, the enemy's deep ranks would reform and come crashing at them. If the attackers continued without pause, he would never stop them, for he could only reach the left flank and not the right flank.

The goblin charioteers and dragon soldiers did not pause, but their steeds did, seeing Nük T'nyr and his Slaedwa bearing down so fast. A brief hesitation, less than a pairing of heartbeats, but it was enough.

Nük T'nyr and his Slaedwa crashed into the dragon soldiers, striking from the side with such force that it carried them through the ranks to the far flank of the pincer, where they met the incoming charioteers. For this, Nük T'nyr's blows flew with fury while he defended against dogs with boot and shield. The forces met with the sound of mountains being rent and sundered.

Then there was a tangle of bodies and a haze of blood fury. He did not know how long the intense fighting lasted, but it seemed an eve, because the sky overhead sank to darkness and then back to light.

He emerged from this driven state to find his battle sword was no longer in his hand. In its place was his shield, which he used to crush, maim and kill, but even this rose and fell with decreasing fury as he found himself with fewer and fewer foes to counter.

Felling the last rider in a bloody field, he took in a few even breaths. He did not know how long he stood there, taking account of himself, but it could not have been long, because behind him the catapults were just releasing another volley and before him the next small rise brimmed with enemy.

His sword, by good chance, rested with its point buried in a great Drakón some ten strides away. Less fortunately, it lay in the direction of the oncoming lines.

He weighed the odds of getting to the sword before he was overrun. Somehow, inexplicably, Kha'el D'erth was at his side, handing him a flask. He took the liquid fire gladly and drank deeply as the two worked their way forward.

"Glory waits for us," he said, his eyes on the sleek, ebony walls of the eternal city some eight leagues distant.

"She does indeed," Kha'el D'erth replied as he retrieved his king's sword from the lifeless Drakón.

Neither got their blades up before the crush of their foe was upon them, and both had to take the first blows on their banded thighs and forearms. The heavy blows were not enough to shatter bones, but they were enough to give both pause. The force of the strikes lit lightning up their legs and backs.

Time resumed its slow crawl. Nük T'nyr saw every movement around him from the sweep of a blade to the raising of an arm in exacting detail. He moved within the sweep of blades yet outside their grasp. He swept right, rending flesh from bone through armor. He crushed back and down with his banded elbow, knocking a warrior from his mount. He took more blows straight on, stepped back, used the edge of his shield to decapitate the onrushers.

He heard shouts behind him, too full of rage for any but his Slaedwa. A hundred Empyrjurin clanged their way forward.

He cried his outrage into the dark sky. His great battle sword ran with blood and his scorn-filled laughter gave his armies renewed hope. The Jurin peoples would rise again.

—

By the eve of the battle's twelfth day, the black walls were but a half league distant. Nük T'nyr, surrounded by his Slaedwa, led the charge toward the gates. Praefect L'kohn and his Scarabaeid followed. To the east and south, Kha'el D'erth's forces held back enemy reinforcements who emerged from waygates that disappeared as suddenly as they appeared. Their force of a hundred and fifty thousand proud Jurins was halved, but they were no less determined.

Once they were within the shadows of the walls, Fhurjurin began tunneling as Styrjurin kissed the heavens with lightning and storm. Monsjurin and Hylljurin kept their places to the rear and continued to batter the city's great structures with their machines of war.

Nük T'nyr spoke a blessing to the sacred eum and to G'rkyr the Merciless, namesake of his heir. Those who defended the space between his forces and the gates were Drakón. While the flyers were his greatest concern, those who walked, crawled, and slithered were no less treacherous.

To his right, Stutk, the Slaedwa Commander of Crims, took a blow that would have sundered any lesser. Nük T'nyr retaliated on the other's behalf with a deep thrust past thick scales to the heart, felling the Drakón even as its great wings beat upon the air seeking escape. Stutk in a blood rage cleft the Drakón's head from its body then raised the severed head with both hands and hurled it over the wall. The dragon's blood was still hissing in the flames of Stutk's flesh when he set upon the next in the line.

Shouting out in glee and praise, Nük T'nyr did likewise. He had only taken a few steps in his charge when an unnatural shift between the heavens and the earth caused him to break off. He looked upward expectantly, and when he did, Praefect L'kohn set upon him. So certain was he of betrayal that his blade was buried in flesh before he could stop himself. An instant later, the heavens shattered as curtains of fire rained down and the earth quaked as it was rent and torn.

It seemed as if Tenhol itself would break. Nük T'nyr steadied himself by digging his blade into the earth and holding on with both hands. Rifts in the earth opened and widened, even as they were filled by burning curtains of slitrain. Blackwind of a thickness and type he had never seen followed, choking and strangling as it went.

"More damned Drakón trickery," Stutk said as he hunkered down beside his king.

Nük T'nyr cursed in rage and frustration, and the blackwinds and slitrains came even harder. "Da'm te nurrin," he said to honor those who died by the hundreds, for even the mightiest of the Scarabaeid could not push these magics aside completely.

He wondered that he and those close to him were untouched only for the quick moment it took him to find Praefect L'kohn and stare into the other's dying eyes. There was a certain satisfaction in those eyes, a smugness that Nük T'nyr understood. "Hurren var de'trod. Kurhri, kurhri, kurhri," Nük T'nyr chanted. Words of the ode to the last free king.

Stutk, matched by Rwenwik, Slaedwa Commander of Kals, stood and took up his king's words. Others followed. Soon the fields were alive with the sounds of the ode lifting over the sounds of death. The Drakón waiting to charge in after the storm ended were met by Jurin with blood and fire racing in their veins.

The fighting continued through the long tolls of the night. Morning found Nük T'nyr with the taste of blood in his mouth. He spat fire as he sought to rally his people. "My father's father lived and died enslaved to the Drakón," he shouted. "Soon we will know freedom and the Drakón will atone for all they have done."

Rwenwik to his left replied before Stutk, even as both matched slitherers fang for fang with their swords, "And we will win. And I will be honored to stand at your side."

"G'rkyr willing," Stutk grunted.

Rwenwik lashed out as he spoke, "I am my own master and the

Merciless will have nothing to do with it, though perhaps D'rk'r the Dark will."

"Indeed," Nük T'nyr shouted as he moved between the two, his blade dancing in his skilled hands.

Kurl'k, L'kohn's former second, was close behind. He paved a path over the rifts and kept stray magics away as the group made their way toward the gates. "L'kohn saved the last," he said quietly to his king. "Your steel, our magic, together as it should be."

"I am more a believer now than ever before," Nük T'nyr said, to settle an old matter between them.

"I am doubly blessed then, and I pledge to you as L'kohn pledged to you."

Nük T'nyr dug in to a particularly large slitherer. Blood and flesh flew as it was hewn. "I accept your pledge, though I still wonder at the need for it."

"Scarabaeid do not go to war with our kings. We choose freely."

Nük T'nyr threw his head back and laughed. "And yet you do. And yet you have for millennia."

"By choice, not by burden of duty."

Stutk shook his head. "All are here by choice, not by burden of duty."

Rwenwik blinked at him, at his boldness. Nük T'nyr voiced approval before the other could speak. "I see how it could seem otherwise given L'kohn's ways and his service with my father. But really—" He stopped, for a sudden exclamation had gone up among the Jurin, a mass cry of rejoicing that moved oddly from the rear.

Nük T'nyr could not see over the black walls, but he could guess at the turn of events that brought such cheers. The tunnelers had broken through—or so he hoped. Hardly feeling his fatigue, his belly light and his thoughts clear, he led another push toward the gates. The press of bodies closed as the Drakón surged forward, and Nük T'nyr's own Slaedwa, eager for more killing, slammed into him as they made their way forward.

Seeing smallfolk now among the Drakón, Nük T'nyr took Grækor in his right hand. With his left hand he drew a short blade from his belt. He worked his way forward with the smaller blade thrust back and angled down to keep the smallfolk from stringing the tendons in his legs, occasionally sweeping it forward to clear a path before his kneecaps.

Suddenly something hit his head so hard his ears rang. Thick claws knotted his hair and his feet were no longer on the ground. He kicked the air as the Drakón drew him up by the scalp. Thinking quickly, he hurled his short blade heavenward, then with Grækor in both hands he thrust up with all his might.

Bellowing, the Drakón dropped him. Nük T'nyr hit the ground, rolled to his feet, and came up with his blade. He killed the beast and went on.

The moment stretched out. He saw every detail, felt every shifting of the air around him. The Drakón slithering before him had teeth as long as his forearm. They glistened white.

He shouted at the repulsive beast, blocked a blow, gave back with his blade. The creature was dark gray, almost black. Its hide was as thick as the best Jurin armor. Its eyes were as big as his fists.

He wrenched his sword from the hide, drove the blade in again and again, trying to work it between the overlapping plates. He grunted satisfaction as hide and scales and flesh parted.

The beast toppled. He ripped his sword free, prepared to move on, but realized there were no more foes between him and the gate. All he could hear were his own heavy breaths.

Everything seemed to stand still. There was a sound like the dry wind that blew through his mountainous homeland. A new tide swept up from behind him, a wall of shouting Jurin, thousands racing forward, and as he looked on, the gates swung open.

He realized he could no longer hold his arms up for more killing, and as his legs gave way, Stutk and Rwenwik caught him.

"You've done it," Stutk said. "The city will be ours by day's end."

"The great ones flee," Rwenwik said, pointing out the mass exodus borne on wings and air ships.

"Not him," Nük T'nyr said. "He will not flee. You'll find him in the lower keep. Go now, take the glory."

—

Stutk and Rwenwik found the Drakón lord just as Nük T'nyr said they would. Nük T'nyr prepared for their return by cleansing himself of blood and sweat and donning his ceremonial armor. They came for him in the middle tolls of the night.

"He waits for you," Stutk said. "You should have been the one to take him. The honor and glory should have been yours."

"Such was not mine to take," Nük T'nyr managed as he stood. "Not just for the one, for the many, for all Jurin."

Nük T'nyr raised his glass to Kha'el D'erth. Kha'el D'erth stood and raised his glass in return. "Strength and resolve."

"Indeed," Nük T'nyr said, emptying his glass. He took his sword from the smith who had cleansed and oiled it, then dismissed those attending him. "Her ladyship?"

"Dead, by his hand I'd expect."

"I'd expect so too."

He left his pavilion with his Slaedwa commanders on either side and Praefect Kurl'k a step behind. He crossed the distance to the inner keep quickly, almost methodically. It was a path he had not forgotten in a thousand cycles. He walked it with his head held high, a sword in his belt and a crown on his head. It was a stark contrast to how he had walked it before at his father's side.

He climbed the bloody steps, entered the keep. Inside his people were making way for him. Having cleaned up the worst of it, they pulled away carcasses to be hacked and hewn. He felt the power in the halls, so much so it was as if they were bathed in magic and not in blood.

Nük T'nyr felt victory in his heart, and knew it was not just a whispered thought when they came to the great hall and saw the great one lying prone on the floor. He was free now no matter what happened from this day forward.

Though he had not spoken, the dragon lord must have sensed his presence. In the hall was writhing and screaming like to wake all the gods. But the sounds did not come from the great one—they came from his sequestered servants.

Nük T'nyr could have brought silence with steel, but instead used words. "Your power is broken, your army is scattered, and your great city is in ruins. I offer exile in place of death."

The Drakón lord fought to a sitting position despite his captors' efforts to keep him prone. He spoke words like a viper swooping in on its prey. The sound that catches you unaware just before deadly jaws snap and venom pumps. "I offer *you* the chance to be raised anew," he said, "A choice for life instead of death."

Nük T'nyr threw back his head and laughed. His laughter echoed throughout the whole of the great hall and beyond. "I am amused at your impudence. At my gesture, you are dead. I will think of you no more than you've ever thought of me or mine."

"Oh, you'll think of me. You'll think of me and you'll curse this day to the end of yours. What you've set in motion cannot be undone. You were born slaves. You will die slaves. You have merely to embrace your new masters."

"I am my own master from this day forward," Nük T'nyr said, and then with his sword he took the thing he had long sought.

The Drakón lord convulsed in response. He did not speak again, though his was a slow death.

Near the end, Nük T'nyr carved out the other's table-sized heart and watched it beat its last beat. He turned to regard his commanders and the praefect with the heart gripped in both hands.

Stutk and Rwenwik fell to their knees. The dozens behind them followed. The hall fell to silence. Only Kurl'k dared to meet Nük T'nyr's gaze.

"They would not give us freedom, so we took freedom for ourselves," Nük T'nyr said. "Today is our Day of Atonement. From this moment forward, we shall know only freedom or death. And death in support of freedom is glory."

The voices raised in reply filled the hall and were almost deafening. A chant of praise issued forth, honoring Nük T'nyr. Nük T'nyr chanted back the name of the most honored fallen. "Ghul Rwern, Ghul Rwern, Ghul Rwern," he began, and he continued through the long list of those who had died bathed in glory.

Daybreak found him in his pavilion, readying the next attack before the enemy could regroup and counting the steps he must take before rising against the next seat of the empire. Kha'el D'erth was there with him through the small hours as were Stutk, Rwenwik, and Kurl'k.

CHAPTER FOURTEEN

Yarr spun around, fearing treachery in the sound of steel behind him, but the Trykathian cavalier and his followers were not threatening him. Instead, he realized they had noticed what he had not—a group of Monsjurin off to the left, walking their way.

They were dressed all alike, in chainmail shirts over crimson robes. They had great widowmaker swords slung across their backs though none had donned their plumed helms.

Xerc resheathed his sword and his followers did likewise. "Guardians of the Wanderer," he said. "The Order of Noble Yrenil."

Yarr nodded and said nothing, but he kept his hand near his sword. While he trusted the flag of respite that flew in the training grounds, he had learned the hard way that nothing was ever as it seemed and nowhere was truly safe.

They stood and waited for the Monsjurin to arrive.

The leader was enormous, with a bushy black beard nearly as long as Yarr was tall. He held up a hand in greeting and spoke in clear Trykathian. Cavalier Xerc answered, and they seemed to have an argument. Then the guardian turned to regard Yarr.

"I am Guardian Jdost," he said, in Cikathian now, "come to battle for honor and glory and freedom. Cavalier Xerc tells me you are a Supremator. I disbelieve."

Yarr held back a grin. None of the Jurin peoples ever came to Cyvair of their own free will. Still, he guessed the alternatives were worse for a warrior people. "I am," he answered.

"It is not possible. I step on you and you are dead."

"That may be so," Yarr said, turning to walk away.

Jdost unsheathed his sword, slammed it into the ground to block Yarr's retreat. The flat edge of the sword was as wide as Yarr himself. The hilt beyond stood several spans above Yarr's head.

Yarr turned back to the Monsjurin, pointed to the drab gray flag flying over the field. "The flag of respite," he said. "No training. No sparring."

"I am promised nine killing days, and on the tenth freedom."

Xerc and his followers moved to stand between Jdost and Yarr. The Trykathians were thick limbed and thick bodied, standing nearly as tall as the gargant's sword hilt, but only half as tall as the gargants. Xerc said, "Rules are as they are."

Jdost and his lot clearly thought otherwise. Jdost took up his sword, shouted, "Coward, coward," and ranted with obscenities.

All conversation in the training ground stopped. Yarr felt a sort of trembling in his soul. "I have told you that the flag of respite flies. I will fight you another day. Our conversation is done."

"You don't walk away from me!"

Yarr, ignoring the gargant's screams and the curses that followed, walked toward one of the few he counted truly a friend.

"Well done," Dhon told him, offering him a place on the bench beside him. "It would shame us all if you were to fight under respite."

Yarr sat next to the hulking Fhurtroll. "I care not of these duties, but I would never purposefully bring shame." He paused, turned to ensure the cavalier and his men were behind him. "Let me introduce you. Cavalier Xerc, this is Dhon of Fetinwol."

Dhon and Xerc clasped forearms. The Fhurtroll and the Trykathian were of a height but the troll's girth was easily twice that of the Trykathian. "I took you for a Trykath slayer. Are you not?"

"I cannot claim that honor. I am but a cavalier."

"It is good to meet you," Dhon said, still gripping Xerc's forearm. "Are you allied with the Dwelmish? They are Goeks, are they not?"

"They are, but we are not allied."

Silence followed. Both Yarr and Dhon had thought all Goeks were allied. It crushed hope.

"Well, I see," Dhon said, breaking the silence. "You are a welcome addition all the same. You join us, do you not?"

"Auy," the cavalier said, and his followers nodded agreement.

The Trojk Master of Keys brought them drink. He was a Trykathian and had won a part of his freedom. The games of the colosseum were his trade. They brought him respect and wealth, much of which was purchased by Yarr's blood and sweat. He honored Yarr when he could, but it was poor substitute for the thing Yarr yearned for. Freedom.

As they drank, Yarr listened to the talk but only participated sporadically. His thoughts were elsewhere, lost to another time and place.

The key master mistook his bliss for something else and whispered, "The new woman, she was good. Yes?"

It took Yarr a moment to return to the here and now. "She was," he said. It was a lie but a small one. The girl was a victory gift, but Yarr did not fight for women or glory. He fought to stay alive. He fought until he need not fight any more. "Send back Rigga. It is her I miss."

"I thought as much," the Master of Keys said. "Rigga it is. She will await your pleasure in the rooms below."

Yarr feigned a smile, which the key master took as genuine. "Thank you, I'll go shortly." He clasped the key master's arm.

He listened to Dhon and Xerc talk. He stayed quiet. The cavalier's followers drank heavily. He did not. Drink clouded thought, slowed response.

When the conversation quieted and the key master had gone, Yarr touched a hand to Dhon's shoulder.

"I will return," he said. "Drink well while I am gone."

Dhon looked at him and smiled knowingly. "I will."

Yarr slid away from the table. He stood quietly out of sight for a short time to ensure all was well with Dhon and Xerc. As he knew they would be, he found the Monsjurin waiting not far off.

—

"Now, I think, we have proper introductions," the enormous Monsjurin said to Yarr. "This is Grekl, my blade whom you've insulted."

"Steel cannot be insulted. It is not a living thing."

"Then you have never met a living blade. This is græsteel, the finest, forged and crafted for my father's father's father at the beginning of time."

Yarr sighed, stepped to the side, prepared himself for the inevitable. "You don't understand. I cannot contest you with steel under the respite flag. The battle that comes is in the colosseum."

"Convenient for you, no doubt, but that's no matter. I'll tear you apart with my bare hands, no steel needed."

Yarr relaxed the muscles of his neck, flexed the muscles of his legs and arms.

Jdost lunged, moving swiftly, more like a colossal ktothian cat than a gargant. Yarr was faster, jumping beyond grasping hands, diving back in to shatter the gargant's front teeth. He continued through, swung around the gargant's head, found himself with his legs about the gargant's neck. He squeezed and twisted. The breath blew out of Jdost and he collapsed.

The other Monsjurin came at him then. From the corner of his eye, Yarr saw a fist. Rather than duck, he jumped up and over, meeting the fist and running up the gargant's arm. He dug into the soft bone at the base of the neck with both elbows. The bone gave way with a splendid crack. The gargant went down.

Another ripped a fence pole from the ground and came at Yarr with it. Yarr ducked, lunged forward, struck groin. The gargant went down, dropping the pole. Yarr picked it up, rolled, and caught his next attacker in the shins. He pulled through with both arms and all his strength, shattering the left shin and bringing screams before the pole broke against the right shin. This brought screaming like all the stars being ripped from the heavens.

Yarr bounded to his feet. He picked up a shard of the pole, shoved it through the flesh of the gargant's throat and out the gaping mouth. This quieted the screaming.

He picked up other shards of the pole. The largest, he drove through a hand that sought to grab him. The smallest, he hammered into a thigh.

No others came at him. He stood his ground, turned a wide circle. It seemed all eyes in the practice yards were on him. The gargants he felled were unmoving. Two others groaned in agony. Jdost panted in a heap on the ground. "Are we done with this?" Yarr asked.

The one left who could still speak said, "It's done."

"I must be going then," Yarr said. "I look forward to our meeting in the colosseum."

He brushed back his hair, swept blood and sweat from his face. Across the yard, he saw the Master of Keys shaking his head in disproval. He walked to him, certain already of the consequences of his actions.

—

"I was provoked," Yarr protested as the master rebuked him.

The Master of Keys led Yarr indoors. "I'm sure ya were, as ever. However, the great ones have declared festival. Games every tenth day for ten to honor the Hundred World alliance. The Jurin were needed."

They entered a narrow tower, crossed a small, private courtyard where the key master remanded his weapons to a hulking Gnog. They proceeded through a waygate, appearing in a dark hallway outside the eating gallery. Yarr stroked his chin. He glanced right.

"How was I to know this? They demanded a fight. I gave one."

The master raised an eyebrow as he walked. "Really?"

"Really. First of all, there were five of them and one of me. The big one, he said I insulted—"

"One dead. One dying. Three injured. Who's to pay?"

"One I only got in the groin, not like I gelded him. The big one, I only choked the air out and loosed a few teeth. The other can't be too bad off, got it in the hand and leg is all. Those other two…Well, they deserved it. Shin-struck was screaming like to wake the gods. That other, might be he was too stupid. Put his big neck right out in front of me."

The old Trykathian frowned. He sat on a bench beside one of the long wooden tables and invited Yarr to do the same. "Still, who's to pay? Them Jurin, they cost a fortune, and where am I to get more? Most Jurin commit kahar'ri or go into blood rages. Either way the same result. Their death before capture and dishonor."

"And I've not made you a fortune these last cycles?"

The Master of Keys scoffed, blew out a breath. "I've not enough coin to cover this up. You've done me in."

Suspicion flitted across Yarr's face. "If so, why didn't you stop it?"

"Like be any could stop ya once ya set your mind to it," the key master muttered. He would have continued, but Rigga appeared carrying an ironstone platter of meat and cheese in bread trenchers, a pitcher of mead, and two tankards.

Yarr regarded Rigga. He touched her shoulder, saw that she was well. Suddenly realizing how thirsty and hungry he was, Yarr downed the tankard, refilled it, and started into the meat and cheese.

The meat tasted of game hen but was from a much larger fowl. The cheese was pungent and buttery. The bread was hard wheat and not strictly for eating, but he ate it anyway. The mead was sweet and tasted of honey and mace but it was not strong, as Yarr preferred to keep his senses and the key master knew this.

He enjoyed the food and drink much too much to find the irony of the meat-eating, ale-drinking Elf he had become. What would his father's father think of him? Would the ancients despise and condemn him? And then a faint whisper of thought: What of Akharran? Would she find him less repulsive?

The key master ate, too. Only Rigga seemed not to notice the food. Her attention was on Yarr. Yarr returned her attention to avoid further conversation, but the old Trykathian spoke anyway. "Order must be kept. I must punish you."

Yarr stared at the other for a moment. "I know this."

"Rules have been broken. I must—" The key master broke off when he seemed to realize Yarr had just agreed with him. He became flustered for a time. Likely, he had planned the argument's turnings beforehand, and Yarr's easy agreement was not something he had foreseen.

Rigga worked her way around Yarr's neck with her lips. She was tall for a human and deeply bronzed by Cyvair's suns. Her fair hair made her a prize of great value, and she once had been his prize for a hundredth win in the colosseum some cycles past. The dim torchlight behind her cast her shadow across the table and made her seem more than she was. A shifter or daemon perhaps, and perhaps she was such, but he had no knowledge of this. He knew her only as Rigga. Once she had told him that she was of the Instra peoples.

There had been pride in her eyes at the saying, but that pride faded and had yet to return.

To break the silence, Yarr said bluntly, "Do what you must. Certainly, I deserve it."

"Jurin," the Master of Keys said, making the word seem portentous. He raised his tankard and drained it; Yarr did likewise. Rigga went to the far side of the gallery to refill the pitcher.

"I'll make it up to you. In the colosseum next time you duel me, I'll take a few blows, let them think I'm done for. You'll get the wagers up and then I'll make a comeback. Like old times."

"Old times are done for, Yarr. Not many are willing to bet against you."

Yarr watched Rigga return. The swing of her hips called his eyes. "The fat one. Surely, the fat one—"

"Speak of the great ones with respect. The big one no longer makes wagers. He is Prince of Praxix now, a ruler of the Hundred Worlds."

"The titan—"

"Comes only to see you dead. You've lost him a fortune. And before you get any ideas of wealth, I get but a handful of brass lokes and copper drudgers for each gold crown traded hands. Lokes and drudgers for me. Crowns for them."

Curled around Yarr's waist, Rigga giggled and kissed his neck. Then she whispered something very quietly in Cikathian. Yarr was too busy filling his cup and the key master's to note exactly what.

"The hunt? It always pleases. Surely there are some great fell beasts to parade and awe. I kill a beast and make amends. All's good."

"The mob grows weary. They lust for blood. Simple kills are no longer enough. We must be more and more refined to please."

"What then?"

"The war with the Jurin goes badly," the Master of Keys said quietly, "The great ones demand a grand spectacle. That's all I know."

"Then give them such spectacle as they will never forget."

The old Trykathian sighed. "They'll only want more."

"Then give them more."

"And if it means the death of all the great Supremators? And if it means your death?"

"I am death."

"That may seem so," the Master of Keys said. "But I've never seen any other fight so hard to live as you."

No more words passed between Yarr and the master. They drank in silence.

With the second pitcher emptied and the mugs drained, the master touched Yarr's shoulder and then left. The touch was a sign of deference. The old Trykathian left Yarr to his pleasures.

Yarr waited until he heard the other enter the waygate, and then he gently stopped Rigga. "He's gone," he said. "You've no more to…" His voice trailed off as he looked up at Rigga. She was straddled across his lap. A smile touched the corners of her lips and there was mischief in her eyes.

"To what?" Rigga asked, just before kissing his lips. "I missed you. It is you I want. You may not believe it, but I do. You are kind and strong and true. No others are this way to me. This one you long for. This Dierá—"

"—Must we?"

"We must. You've said yourself it was others who wanted you to be together and promised you each to the other. You have never been with her. You've been with me, and yet it is her you think of."

Yarr lifted Rigga away and up to a seat on the tabletop. "I can never be what you want me to be, Rigga. Dierá is hope, and together we are the vitality of my people."

Rigga leaned forward and whispered. "I do not ask you to be anything. I ask only that you be with me in this moment. This moment is what we have. The rest may never be."

Yarr could not argue with the logic of her words. He returned her kisses and soon her caresses.

CHAPTER FIFTEEN

"G'rkyr, G'rkyr, where are you?" Dierá called out as she ran. She peaked behind a large couch upholstered in golden silk and threaded with the visages of majestic birds, continued toward her bedroom suite with its canopied bed and wide, wide windows. She entered, saw the curtains move, and was certain the other was hiding behind them. She jumped to the window and pulled the curtains back, only to find the windows were open and the movement was the wind playing.

Bright sunlight streaming in through the window caused her eyes to lose their focus. She had to wait a moment before she could return to her search among the shadows of her apartments. She stood absolutely still, listening. "Come out, I know you're there. I know where you are," she cried out, though in truth she did not.

A voice returned, sounding far away and small, and a smile lit her face. She hurried off, racing into the dressing closet, jumping to the pile of clothes that spoke and moved, knowing it was her G'rkyr.

"G'rkyr, G'rkyr," she said. "Come out, come out, my love."

G'rkyr emerged from the clothes pile. He saw Dierá and laughed. "I picked the best spot. How did you find me?"

Dierá hid a smile with her hand. "I just knew."

He reached out and touched her ear with a hand that was almost as big as hers was now. "It must be this. You hear a hoppish a field away with this."

"Ear," Dierá said in the language of the Élvemere.

"Ear, ear," G'rkyr repeated excitedly, also in Elvish.

Dierá hugged him and kissed both of his cheeks. He squealed with delight.

"Come now," Dierá said. She took his hand and led him into the talking room, laughing with delight at the sound of his bare feet against the wood floor.

She seated him at a study table in the far corner, took the chair beside him. "Shall we?" she asked, though her voice made it clear it was more command than question.

G'rkyr frowned. "Father says Jurin need not learn reading and writing."

Dierá tickled him. "Well then, maybe you are not Jurin?"

"I am no Alv."

It was Dierá's turn to frown. "That word again. The Élvemere are every bit as worthy of being named as such."

"Sorry, mother," G'rkyr said with a quick smile, and Dierá knew she could never truly be angry with him. "Tell me the story of the red ktoth. Please. Please."

"It is Jurin lore. Today's lesson is—"

"Father says lore and credo and law are all I must ever know."

A chill ran down Dierá's spine as he began to chant,

Kurhri da'm te nurrin var ma'hdden
Kurhri adda'tten te garran var sa'dron
Kurhri mo'rren te hurre var de'trod
Serfre do dedon terra sur varahet
Serfre do treten furra sur kovnat
Serfre do motroten kirra sur ptlock.

She harbored hope the lusting could be nurtured out, but his little face as he sang lit with such delight and purpose. He did not just speak the words, he believed them as deeply and sincerely as his father believed them. She swallowed a mother's grief, kept the tears from her face, the tremble from her voice. "Very nice. So it is the ktoth again?"

"Yes, please. The red ktoth."

"The one who drowned the world and walks the night sky?"

"That one!" G'rkyr exclaimed with a squeal of delight.

It was a little thing, that show of joy and pleasure, but it was enough. She clung to it as she began. "Only one beast rules the night, and that beast is the ktoth of Nall. Red he is from nose to tail and fierce he is from tail to nose. No Drakón or titan or Jurin could stand singly against him, for he is without equal, without fear."

"But," G'rkyr interrupted.

"But there was one," Dierá said, laughing. "One who stood alone against the mighty ktoth of Nall."

"And?"

"And his name Kvar, King of Kings and Jurin born," said a deep voice from across the room.

Little G'rkyr looked up, ran to his father. Big G'rkyr grabbed up his son with one hand, and the two thumped heads in greeting. This brought laugher as ever, but it was not laughter filled with scorn and contempt and it strengthened Dierá's hope.

—

Bright light struck and a face appeared as if in sunrise. It was an Empyrjurin face, but it was not little G'rkyr.

At first she saw only his questioning eyes. They were so dark a red and so reflective that she could see herself in them as clearly as if she stared into a looking glass. They were the eyes of death and of life.

She blinked, stared. It took her a moment to realize the light was from living fire burning in flesh and not from the pale yellow suns of the accursed world that was now her home.

"Can you sit up?" he asked. His voice was all husk. His large hand enveloped her shoulders as he helped her sit up.

Living fire faded and his eyes became dark pools beneath his bulging brows. Now she saw his strong face, with broad cheekbones carved of granite and hair like straw, but as red as the living fire itself. In her eyes his stern face had a rugged handsomeness to it now, and softness too that perhaps she alone knew of.

Behind G'rkyr enormous glass doors lead away from the balcony, and beyond an alabaster railing everything was enveloped in shadow. Confusion gripped her. She was lying on a red, satin sunlounger, wearing a dress of saffron chenille with golden threading. The cut and thickness of the dress helped to show off her gentle curves, but it was the graceful, reserved movements that made the dress and her seem alluring. She shifted her gaze about the furnishings of the large room and knew she was in one of the sitting rooms.

"Be calm," he said. "You are wakeful, though not entirely well. You dream I think. Morning is nearly upon us." His free hand went to a ceramic pitcher that was rounded and sized for easy handling by Jurin and Alv alike. He poured the contents into a glass.

She used both hands to drink from the large glass. "It is the dream, always the same. It haunts—"

"It does not matter. Karthold is behind us, as I promised you."

She shifted her legs, leaned toward him. "All is set in motion then?"

"It is, Dierá."

She felt the color return to her face. "And he—"

G'rkyr knelt at her side. "I have forsaken everything for you, yet he is all you can think of. Is it enough? Will it ever be enough? Will I ever be enough?"

Like dew turned to frost, her expression hardened. "How dare you!" she screamed. "I forswore all that is sacred. I have lain with you, and it disgusts me to think of your pleasure soaking me. A thousand, thousand deaths for me if any others should ever know. I am a queen of my people. A queen of queens…"

He tried to speak. She cut him off with the ice in her eyes. He touched her gently, enveloping the whole of her back with his hand. She recoiled from his touch. It revolted her. Surely, any others watching would only see the monstrousness of this thing between them.

He raised a finger to her cheek, gave it a delicate stroking. She quietly seethed, closing her eyes against the gentleness that only she knew.

Loathing was there as ever, but that loathing was directed inward. His gentle touch overwhelmed her sensibility. It revolted her and yet attracted her. He was a monster of fire and stone, incapable of feeling by his own admission, and yet he felt and loved, just as she felt and loved.

White-hot tears in her eyes were followed by her fists in his chest. "The impossibility of it all. Jurin and Alv. That I love you! That I hate you! That I am saved. That I am damned. The absurdity…The absurdity of it all…"

She embraced him, her outstretched arms barely reaching across his abdomen. Her love for him was real but she knew not to succumb to the illusion. Focus, find resolve, she told herself, but she could not. Her heart raced. Her thoughts ran wild. She had pursued glimmers and ghosts, grasped air and dream, sold herself and her soul for whispers.

None of that would matter if the rumors were true. Finally, she would be in the right place at the right time. Then there would be no more searching, no more scheming, no more despair of all hope being lost. The search would be at an end. Hope would be restored to her people, but what of herself would remain?

She dared not think or say his name lest dream and hope collapse upon the crush of reality. Yet she had dared hope before and had dared his name before, only to have it all taken away. "Set in motion. Are you sure?" she asked, her eyes pleading, her voice scarcely a whisper.

G'rkyr nodded. "Steel yourself, Dierá. Dry the tears. Find the resolve you always search for." He shrouded his body in living flame. Fire hid all trace of emotion. She sucked in air that seemed suddenly stifling, collected herself by wiping tears from her eyes, straightening her dress, and smoothing back her hair. "Bring him," he commanded.

It took three pair of the yellow-skinned, bug-eyed luvens to open the great glass doors. Behind them, Nostik, Keeper of the House, ushered in Zanük and a squad of Fedwëorgs clad in field regalia. Towed and chained in their midst was one of the ageless. Size alone told Dierá this Drakón was special. The great curved horns ringed from base to tip were an unexpected extra. They told her this one was of the line.

"He is Takhbarre Battikh, Prince of Praxix," Zanük told her in Jurin.

Dierá dismissed Zanük and the others, turned herself so her full figure showed in profile. Behind her, the rising yellow suns told of morning's arrival. "Takhbarre, we can begin our discussion in shadow or light," she said. There was no hint of apprehension in her voice but she knew her scent betrayed her. The language she chose was Cikathian. It was the language of slaves.

Focus, find resolve, she told herself. Hiding emotions from her scent was proving difficult, but she was confident she would be able to master this now that she knew scent was why Drakón always saw her true intentions.

Pulling G'rkyr's strength over her, she thrust herself and the Drakón into shadow. The domain she created was a hollow large enough to grant herself free movement yet small enough to deny the Drakón his wings. Beyond the hollow was darkness that made the silver glow from her gray eyes seem like lamp fire.

"You will show me how to touch The Abundance. You will tell me of him, the Undying One, and more," she said. Her voice though calm carried an implied threat. For his part, the Prince of Praxix curled his spiked tail around his folded wings. The position seemed to speak of his submission to her strength, but she knew one could never be certain with a Drakón. They were a breed apart, and every bit of their being was designed to rule over all things. It was this need to dominate that she would need to weed out. It was what the long struggle would be all about.

Predictably, the Prince of Praxix made his move in the moments that followed, testing the bounds of the hollow and her resolve to hold its balance. She fought back, a hard scrabble to keep the fabric of the hollow intact. Raw magic raged from her outstretched fingers, her eyes, and her gaping mouth, crackling and sparkling with the blue-white intensity of the hottest flame.

She felt her strength ebb and flow. Her reserves spent and certain unconsciousness was coming, she reached out beyond shadow to G'rkyr. His eum centers were wellsprings, and he opened himself to her. The raw energy flowed in great waves from him to her. Only this connection to G'rkyr kept her strength.

The tocks of the toll flowed. Tolls flowed into night. Night became day.

After a while, it seemed the swells and falls were all Dierá had ever known. Great upsurges followed by brief ebbs. Agony followed by numbness. The endless and the fleeting.

When Takhbarre finally submitted, Dierá was left gasping, shocked, and awed. Free thought returned first, followed by feelings beyond pain and numbness. She fought to keep her feet but failed.

The world suddenly was dulled. There was a great absence, a void. She needed to fill this void. Her link to G'rkyr was severed. She was alone.

Desperately, she reached out beyond shadow, found only emptiness. Panic followed. Her mind raced. She had never before drawn so much.

Her resolve faltered. "G'rkyr, G'rkyr?" she called out across the link.

She felt the shadow world fall away, clung to it. Her concern turned into anger, her anger into rage.

Takhbarre raised his front quarters, brought his long neck around his folded his wings. "What you ask I cannot do. You cannot understand this thing you seek. It would consume you. No matter how many times we dance in shadow the answer will be the same."

It was a lie. The lie gnawed at her. Rage gave her renewed resolve and strength. If G'rkyr was dead, she had nothing to lose. "We dance in shadow as many times as it takes. If it means your end, if it means my end, that's what it means."

Focus, find resolve, she told herself. *Just knowing the struggle of the long cycles could be at an end should be enough.* "Tell me," she commanded in the language of the ageless. As she spoke, she folded light into shadow and returned to the waking world. There she found G'rkyr and hope.

"Whispers, whispers," the great Drakón replied. This brought G'rkyr's full fury as he himself took up the binding chains. He shouted, "Tell her what you told me or I'll end you."

The Drakón fought to throw off his chains, but G'rkyr

contained him. "I am ageless," the Drakón hissed, "You are not Scarabaeid. You are Werrsweord." As he said this, the Drakón shifted to shadow. His surprise at finding Dierá waiting for him was palpable. It was her domain he came to, and not the one he had sought to reach.

—

Dierá glared at the enormous Drakón. She dared not think or say the name on her lips, lest dream and hope collapse upon the crush of reality. Yet she had dared hope before and had dared his true name before, only to have it all taken away. "The Undying One?" she demanded, collapsing the shadow space inward, forcing a withdrawal from shadow.

"Cyvair," hissed the Drakón, eyeing Dierá furtively.

If he lives, my people live—and as she thought this, she again became the queen of queens that she was breed to be. "Among the ageless there are whispers?"

"Whispers within whispers."

"And they love him?"

"Adulation of the mob is not love." As Dierá pulled G'rkyr into shadow with her, the Drakón's demeanor changed. He curled his tail and lowered his wings. "It is said he has died a thousand deaths and yet lives."

"How?" she demanded. It was one word, and a simple one at that, but it carried the weight of the long struggle.

"Unknown," the other hissed in reply. "It is not the rebirthing. Only the Drakón can be reborn. Perhaps, rusecraft. If so, as dark and vile as ever there was. Makhatar calls him the Soulless One."

Dierá stood as tall and as regally as any queen ever had or ever would. "If soulless, I will ensoul him. I will do this for my people."

"Your people are no more," the Drakón sneered.

"He is my people," Dierá replied, and then she turned to G'rkyr, saying, "End him now."

"When I am reborn I will find you, Athania Dierá Steorra. Time and distance will not hide you from me."

"From shadow there can be no rebirth," Dierá said. In shadow, she gave G'rkyr the signal to continue. The gargant obeyed, pulling taught the chains around the Drakón's neck.

The Drakón flailed and fought. His will to live was no surprise to Dierá. When her point was made, she stayed G'rkyr's wrath with a raised hand.

The Drakón gasped, "I am Prince of Praxix, a ruler of the Hundred Worlds. I am better alive than dead, a better friend than foe. Kill me and you will never have the thing you seek. Let me live and there is chance."

"You would betray us."

"Likely, and given opportunity, a certainty. This I will not deny, but you need me more than you know. All the armies of the Hundred Worlds could not breach the defenses of Cyvair. It is our homeworld, and we defend it until the last of us falls still."

"Of this, I'm certain," Dierá said, her upturned eyes never leaving the Drakón's. "Tell us then how we breach defenses that cannot be breached."

"I cannot."

"Show me The Abundance!"

"I cannot."

Dierá clenched her hands into fists as her face flushed red with all the rage she was feeling. At times she felt she was Empyrjurin, and this was one of those times. "End him, G'rkyr, or so help me—"

The Praxixian Prince lowered his front quarters while raising his neck in a rare show of supplication. "This is something that I can show, but not tell. Drakón can do what is required. Others cannot."

"We'll see about that," Dierá countered, pulling herself and the others out of shadow.

Clearly taken aback by the ease with which she moved from and to shadow, the Drakón said, "You, Athania Dierá Steorra, are full of surprises. You master shadow in ways only Drakón can. Perhaps you are right about the Soulless One. Perhaps, you can ensoul him. I shall want to live to see this, if no more. Return my endowments and I will gladly dance with you in shadow."

"You live only if Dierá says you live," grunted G'rkyr. "Here she is god, and you are but mortal."

"You need me," cautioned the prince. His great eyes locked on Dierá's. "He is Jurin Werrsweord. You need more than the Scarabaeid and Slaedwa at his command for this thing you plan."

Feeling the presence, Dierá's thoughts spun and she called out without words. *You are stronger than I dared hope.*

The prince responded in kind. *Is that how it works? You command and he searches the worlds for you?*

It is as it is. Dierá returned.

The son is not the father. He can never be what you hope for. Why do you think you are remanded to the farthest edge of the Hundred Worlds? You are kept as far from the true power as possible. The Jurins will never trust you but we can—

Dierá thrust the Drakón out of her thoughts, said aloud, "It is as it is."

The prince hurled his will back into Dierá's mind, found only the walls she constructed for him. Feeling more secure, Dierá sat on the edge of the sunlounger with her back straight and her eyes uplifted to the Drakón's. "Tell me why you should be allowed to live?"

"I am here to offer the thing you seek."

"You are here, because *you* are the thing I sought."

The prince's sudden laughter shook the floor. "None command the ageless, least of all an Alv and a Jurin."

G'rkyr leapt upon the Drakón. His great hands with their long, thick fingers wrapped about the Drakón's throat. "You are commanded to submit and cease speaking."

If only it were so easy, the Drakón whispered in thought to Dierá.

"Enough," Dierá said, sending G'rkyr back with a wave of her hand.

G'rkyr glowered a double stride away, his eyes never leaving the prince's form even when Nostik entered to announce the squads of Fedwëorgs who were just returning from the battlefields through the waygates. Dierá took in the bloodied commanders, the laden chests, the faithful who bent their knee heedless of their wounds. A great victory was the thing their bearing spoke of. Though they remained silent, Zanük's presence in the hall shadows confirmed a conquest.

G'rkyr was their commander, but it was Dierá they looked to. She stood, walked among them. Though the Fedwëorgs continued to kneel, they reached out to her as she went by. She touched those whose need was greatest, pulling the gravest of their wounds from them and into her.

The pain of this exchange, this taking of death and giving of life, brought her to her knees many times. At these times, the wounds she took in were her own and she wore them openly, but she maintained her walk among the squads until she reached the farthest ranks. Here it was G'rkyr's will and G'rkyr's will alone that allowed her to keep her feet and walk with steady determination back to the sunlounger. Through it all, she took of G'rkyr's strength as much as she dared. By the time she sat and resumed her scrutiny of the Prince of Praxix, she was again herself. G'rkyr, on the other hand, could hardly keep his feet, but he hid his weariness well.

"Indeed, full of surprises," the prince said. "Your mastery of light is as strong as your mastery of shadow. Both things you wanted me to know."

Dierá's gaze focused on the prince alone even as G'rkyr dismissed the squads and Nostik showed the warriors the way out. "These are the deepest of my gifts, and I lay them bare so that you may know me as I will come to know you."

She waited until certain there was clear understanding between herself and the prince, then she told G'rkyr, "Remove him. Send in Nostik." To Nostik, she said, "Fetch the young ones."

Exhausted as she was, she felt like celebrating this victory. The young ones she referred to were her musicians. Her discovery of the luven's aptitude for music pleased her immensely. Theirs was a natural talent. She put it to use playing the romantic operas her father so loved.

The luvens' glass and wind instruments helped her recreate the most haunting theme imaginable—that of Veden's *50th Summer,* which drew together the romantic ideas of love and death and played on the contact between the natural world and the worlds beyond. The power of storm was in that music as was the strength of earth.

Her favorite instrument was the glass organ with its pedals and spinning bowls. The luvens secreted a sweet fluid from their hands; they used this to keep their fingers wet while they played the spinning bowls. When stroked just right, the sounds that sprang forth evoked images of wind blowing across fields, down rivers, and through forests. It was transcendent, sublime.

Dierá had not heard music played so beautifully since her mother lived. Her mother played the concert harp in ways that moved listeners to tears; luvens achieved as much with their simple winds and odd glass. She fell asleep even before the luvens finished the first movement.

CHAPTER SIXTEEN

Yarr heard a faint shifting and slipped his eyes open a touch, reluctant to leave the drau world where Dierá called to him. He saw the white bone first, sharpened and made into a blade. The hand that held it next. *The new ones are a danger to themselves,* he thought to himself. "To slit my throat, you'll need to move quieter, Arger," he said in the Rweng language, making no move to defend himself.

The other replied in the same blunt tongue. "Scaet, if I wanted you dead you'd be. I want you afeared is all."

Yarr sat up. "I'm sure wat not as it may."

"Mock, scaet, while you've wind to dwy it."

In one swift, fluid movement, Yarr reached out, gripped the other's wrist, and turned the blade back to its owner's neck. "I told you. I did what the masters wished. Nothing more. Twinnit?"

The fire in Arger's eyes increased. "Uog was as brother to me. Slit my throat if you must for I will slit yours when I've a chance."

Yarr dropped the sharpened bone to the floor, leaned back with an arm behind his head. "Let me go to my dreams. I will kill you soon enough. Then you can join Uog."

"Death, is it so easy to your hand?"

"It is."

"More's the pity. Auy. I will see Rwe again. I will walk its paths. Erland is my homeland. Wat where I will die."

Yarr responded by closing his eyes. He heard the tall Erlander pick up the bone knife and tuck it into the back of his pants. Then the other retreated to the opposite corner of the cell. *Go,* he told the other in his thoughts. *I have no need of you.*

He had pledged to stop trying to befriend those the ageless put in the cells with him. It was easier to kill them when the time came if he did not know them, and the time for death always came. He had no control over it. He had no control over anything or anyone.

Only thoughts of Dierá kept him. She was the whisper, the thought, the dream that staved off madness. Often he wondered if she was real and not a thing conjured of a need. He conjured his mother and father of a need. They spoke to him from the blessed land. At times he even walked with them in Élvemere—the place that was also whisper, thought, dream.

Though he had long since been unable to, he tried to see Dierá's face. He saw her form in his mind's eye, caught snatches of her voice in his ear, yet there was no substance to any of it, and her face remained as elusive as ever.

Yarr focused, tried again to see Dierá's face. She called to him. Only something was different. Something was changed. For a fleeting moment, he thought the voice was that of Akharran, as the Wërg queen was ever with him. Of all the faces hers was one he had not forgotten, and he always could see her clearly. But the voice was from without and not from within.

"Arger," he said without opening his eyes. "I told you I would kill you later, but if you persist—"

"Yarr, it is I, Martin. Martin of Voethe."

Yarr went to the bars of his cell, looked out at the dark-haired man of Voethe. "What passes?" he asked.

Martin replied in the language of the Élvemere, "You'd know yourself if you could bite your tongue."

Purposefully, Yarr replied in the language of the Kingdoms of Men, "It is not in me to submit or kneel. I know not why, I only know that I cannot."

"Then you will rot in this cell."

Yarr cast glum eyes to Arger in the far corner. The angry Erlander spoke Rweng and little else. "Tell your masters to return. I am ready to go to the pit."

"I will not. It would mean your death. You fought yesterday— and they are your masters as well as mine."

"I have no masters. I am death."

—

To task, Martin told himself. *The dream, the plan. Plans within plans.* He stopped midstride, turned, grabbed at Yarr through the bars but Yarr was too quick for him. "Will you stop this foolishness? I pledged for you and you've brought me nothing but misery. Would you prefer if I left you to die?"

"I am dead. I am unseen. You are too, only you refuse to accept your fate."

"Truly? When I do not breathe, I want for air. When I do not eat, I hunger. When I do not drink, I thirst. You take breaths same as me. You must eat and drink same as me."

"Death is mine, I am hers. I've her marks to prove it," Yarr said, pointing to the lines etched in the near wall.

"I've long since known the marks were not to track the passing of days," said Martin. "You mark death to take account and find absolution, and if you must know, I've judged you and found you not wanting. You take no joy, no revelry, in it.

"You knew I was no soldier. You and you alone kept me alive in this place when all others would have left me to die. Within you beats a kind heart. I believe in you even if you've long since stopped believing in yourself."

Though he did not reply with words, Martin saw an answer in Yarr's eyes. That answer was pain. Pain as deep and profound as the deepest of rivers, and that pain ran through Yarr, devouring him. "Submit. It is all the masters ask. Bend your knee. Kiss your blade. Swear your oath."

Yarr spat. "There's to your oath."

Martin grabbed at Yarr through the bars. Yarr made no move to step away. "You are as brother to me. If I had but half your gifts, I could rule Cyvair in ten cycle's time *with* the masters' blessings, and yet you waste your talents as you waste your life. Look at me, Yarr, I have aged.

"My beard grows thick and full if I wish it. My father would say it means I am a man now. Yet you have not aged a day. You look the same as you did five winters past.

"Do you not understand that my people are not long lived? I

must live a lifetime in the span you say is but a turning of the hand. I will die of old age before you enter the full depth of your manhood—if you live that long and do not die here in this place."

Yarr took a step back as Martin released him. "You don't know how old I am, Martin. Don't presume that I am not yet of a full age."

"I've seen others of Élvemere. Cyvair is rife with them. If you ever get beyond this cage, you'd see that too. Perhaps you'd even find some of Lekloren."

"You know I can't." Yarr said nothing of the grave danger in such; this was unspoken but implied. He had never purposefully told Martin who he truly was, though Martin had learned it. They had shared the cell for several cycles and Martin had brought him back from death once. Any other, Yarr likely would have killed to keep such a secret—or simply let die when the opportunity arose, which it often did, but Yarr trusted Martin and Martin trusted him.

"If ever I was of Voethe, you are of Lekloren. Your fair hair and steel gray eyes, your build, your idioms—all these things declare it to all who see you if they know anything of the Hundred Worlds."

With a soft focusing of the way and will, Yarr changed the color of his eyes to a deep rich red. The color of blood and crimson. His price for using the forbidden was pain, which Martin watched him fold into the pain he already wore as if a shroud. "I was told once that nothing happens by chance. Perhaps there is a reason I must be in this 'cage,' as you call it."

"The only reason is your pig-headedness."

"This 'pig' you are so fond—"

"A beast with…with…You know this…" Martin's voice trailed

off as he saw the faraway look in Yarr's eyes—the look that told him Yarr was no longer in the here and now. He clenched his hands in fists and stalked off, returning to his duties. Chasing tears from his eyes, he looked back and shouted out in Cikathian, which served as a common language in Cyvair, "Die then. Your death is as nothing to me."

In his haste to get away, Martin knocked into the Trojk Master of Keys and a book fell out of his inside pocket. He scooped it up, stood and met the master's eyes. This possession brought a capital punishment. Martin knew this and yet he willingly risked it. When the Trykathian looked the other way, Martin knew what Yarr also knew in that instant. Yarr was being called forth. The pit awaited.

As if in unspoken answer, the Master of Keys opened Yarr's cell and called him forth. Then the Master of Keys called Arger forth.

Martin's step quickened as he raced away. *There's time yet,* he told himself. *This thing that comes can be turned away—it must be.*

—

Yarr stepped out of the cell. He watched Martin recede down the long, straight corridor, resolved that he would never tell Martin the real reason he preferred the pit to the master's halls. In the pit, all were enemies and no one had yet proven his match. In the master's halls, his enemies would have the faces of friends and rusecraft would bring his end. Better to be Yarr, the pit fighter, than Rastín Dnyarr Túrring, the dead son of a dead king from a dead land.

He walked alongside the Master of Keys. Arger followed a step behind. The master was a tall Trykathian with a girth more akin to an ancient oak than anything else. Though oafish in appearance, he was kind, and Yarr never made the mistake of underestimating him as others did. In battle, Trykathians were fearless and their thick skin gave them great advantage. One did not slash and slice a Trykathian. One stabbed and hacked a Trykathian, and hoped to dig deep enough to draw blood.

"Listen closely," the old Trykath said. His voice was almost a whisper, though it did not need to be for Yarr was certain Arger could not speak Cikathian. Uog knew not a word of it—even after a turning of trying to learn it, hadn't. The language was simply too foreign to his tongue and ears. "This is the second and final day, but soon a tenday of games comes. The spectacle marks the rising glory of Makhatar. Survive the stage this day and you will still die. It is divine will."

Yarr did not speak. Instead, he counted his steps. The maze of tunnels between the pits and cells were impossible to navigate otherwise. By the count and turnings he knew the key master led him to the far side. He would be close to the masters at the start of it. This meant the one who called him forth wanted to know or study him—or perhaps watch him die.

"Yesterday's spectacle was as nothing. This battle you will play at is where the death of your people began as surely as it is where the divine's rise began."

Yarr's thoughts turned dark, to the coming fight and the bloodletting. Death comes for us all, he told himself. Embrace death to live. To the master, he said, "I will not die because of anyone's wish."

"The whisperers have turned the mob against you. They say you are soulless, that you must die for the glory of the Hundred Worlds."

The Trykathian stooped down, circled through his keys. Yarr

took a step back and away. It was here at the pit doors that the desperate tried to overwhelm the key master. Yarr's act told the old master that he had no intention of doing such a thing.

The same was not true of Arger. This was his first time to the pits. He knew of them from Uog and feared his own mortality.

Yarr watched Arger slip the bone knife from its hiding place. Arger reeked of fear. Fear no doubt controlled him.

Arger stepped in with his blade, reaching for a place in the Trykathian's back. Yarr jumped, brought his elbow down on Arger's arm, followed up with a knee to Arger's chin.

Arger dropped the knife, stepped back, hands held to his bloody mouth. "I'll kill you, scaet."

"Likely not."

Arger took a swing at Yarr. The Master of Keys shoulder -butted him into the pit. Yarr picked up the bone knife, slipped it into a calf pocket in his hidepants. The Trykathian bobbed his head in thanks as Yarr stepped into darkness.

The Trykathian closed the door, whispered to Yarr as he did so. His words in Cikathian. "One above all others has come to see your death. He is titanus."

The light from the doorway shrank to a sliver. Yarr nodded, looked out at the master from the darkness. The Master of Keys reached into the darkness with his words. "Tolleck block will be empty without you."

Yarr grinned, certain the words were as close to kindness as the Trykathian could offer. He looked up, no sadness or regret reflected in his eyes. "My bones are yet my own."

"Auy, agreed," the Master of Keys said. He handed Yarr a gilded coin or token of a sort, carved with the image of a lady. "She is Beqheth, Mother of the Warrior. She will keep you if any can."

Yarr nodded his thanks, gripped the charm in his fist. The thick rounded metal felt cool against the flesh of his palm. He secured the charm in a hidden pocket partway up the tight sleeves of his hideshirt. The Master of Keys closed and locked the pit door.

When his eyes adjusted to the darkness, he saw the pit in its entirety. The weapons and armor cache were in the middle of the chamber. Allowing him into the pit before the others was a courtesy the master gave him. Although Erlanders could not see in the dark as those of Élvemere, Arger had already helped himself to its contents. Yarr told the other, "Cast off that heavy shield and helm. They'll do you no good."

Arger spat, swung the shield in a wide arc. "You only want them for yourself."

"They are overweighted, poorly made. They'll slow you down. You'll find your end sooner."

"You are no friend to me. I'll take my chances."

Yarr sifted through mostly poorly made goods for the stupid and the weak, found a sword with good balance, a serviceable dagger, and a spear with a sharp tip. "I was friend to Uog, who you said was as brother to you. He died with honor, and it was not my will to bring his end."

"Rwe waits for me. I will walk its paths to Erland before my spirit rests, and then I will go to Aegot."

"Aegot doesn't even know you exist—" Yarr edged toward the other as he spoke. "—and your spirit will be traveling sooner than you think. Might as well take you to Rwe myself." His words ended as he struck out with his fists. His first blow crushed the Erlander's nose. His second boxed the side of the Erlander's head.

The Erlander staggered forward, crying out into the darkness. "Scaet, your death comes."

Yarr jumped up, thrust down into the small part at the base of the other's throat with both elbows. This brought Arger to his knees, where Yarr's well-placed kick found the side of his head, sending him to the dirt in a heap. Arger was in pain but mostly intact.

"I told you the helm and shield were useless." Yarr stripped Arger of the armor, tossing both helm and shield away before thrusting the spear, dagger, and sword into the ground at the other's feet. "Use the spear to stave off the first charge. If you still draw breath, use the sword. Use the dagger at the last for the close work."

Arger looked up, both hands held to his nose to stem the flow of blood. "Why crush me and then help me?"

"You Erlanders are here only for the blood count. You are plentiful and die quickly. The crowd likes it. I like to remind the masters that even those they deem weak can be strong. So be strong, Erlander, and perhaps you will live through this day. Then perhaps, when it is your time, Aegot will know you as I'm certain he knew Uog."

—

The machines awoke with the whines of their pulleys. The earth trembled. The floor of the pit began to rise. Yarr readied himself.

The light came. A sliver at first, then a shaft. Soon Yarr could see beyond the darkness. He spread his arms wide, hefting a spiked chain in one hand, a long-headed spear in the other.

The gathered masses came alive. Yarr turned a wide arc. His eyes found his foes while his mind took the balance of each.

He felt the presence then, a soft touch at the back of his thoughts. It spoke without speaking, telling him who had come to see his death.

He answered as ever with action, showing the watcher that death would find others and not him.

CHAPTER SEVENTEEN

Martin looked back one more time before mounting the stairs, certain he was about to lose the only friend he had known in accursed Cyvair. He clutched the book in his hands before returning it to the inside pocket. Tears were gone from his eyes and would not come again, for he would not let them. He resolved to be strong, though he suddenly felt utterly alone.

Yarr had kept him alive, brought him back from the brink many times, never asking for payment. He had saved Yarr once, true, but only once. A counter to the hands full of times Yarr had saved him.

Yarr needed a different kind of saving now. The Elf needed to know something other than hatred and death, even if only at the very last.

The sounding of the fourth toll of morning put haste into his step. The masters would wake soon and all must be in place. As Day Master of Hearth, his work carried him to the kitchens, to the great halls, to the bedchambers of masters and guests, to the stockyards, and on occasion to the fields and cells.

Hearth slaves were mostly Gnogs, though some few were men and elves. Gnogs were indigenous to Cyvair. They were to be used in the yards and fields but never to be seen within the stone walls. He knew not why. Decisions and choices were the dominion of the masters. It was not his place to question. His place was to ensure things were done, and done properly. Obtaining order from chaos was something he was good at. The reason he was what he was. The reason he was not in a cell beside Yarr.

Martin navigated a league of corridors, keeping mostly to the slave runs. He found the Gnog Prime in the yards as expected. He grunted and smacked his head against the prime's upturned fist as was Gnogish custom on greeting, coming away with his forehead covered in burnished scales. He surveyed the mountains of tree trunks, watched as the Gnogs turned trunks into man-sized fire logs, listened as the prime grunted orders.

There was no animosity between Gnogs and men but there was no true friendship, either. Martin knew his place, worked to build rapport as he could. The Gnog Prime, Kgnrsh, seemed to respect this, and so far had caused Martin no troubles.

"Cvnd zdhs," the Gnog Prime finally told him, and Martin nodded agreement. He was later than usual. It was almost five tolls.

Martin touched five fingers to his right palm, said, "Crknk." He drew a circle, touched three fingers to his right palm, said, "Zdrwn." He touched four fingers to his right palm twice, said, "Frrxth." These were orders for logs to the halls, bedchambers, and kitchens respectively. The great halls needed warming logs. The bedchambers needed day logs. The kitchens needed logs aplenty for the morning cook fires.

The skin of his arms began to burn, and he looked up with disdain at the bright red trisuns of Cyvair. He hurried back into shadows within the stone walls, working his way to the kitchen complex, which was housed on a level of its own and served much of the city. This meant he went east of the slave towers, past the colosseum, and then down below the lower passageways. He had long since stopped marveling over the feats of engineering that created such places—the entire city was an engineering marvel—but especially the kitchens, for they were connected below ground, seemingly to every habitable structure in the city.

In the Varthen kitchen, Tandy, a thick-hipped, yellow-skinned and bug-eyed Begreth, waited for him as ever. "I've ordered the morning logs. Any feasts or banquets that I don't know of?"

Tandy eyed him, ladled a large helping of something from a cook pot. "Quiet, eat," she told him. Martin looked to the fires in the kitchen hearths. Tandy set a bowl and a satchel before him. "The work will wait."

Martin slipped the book to Tandy as he sat. She scooped it up and hid it away. He drank in the aroma wafting from the steaming bowl, picked up the spoon and started to shovel. The hearty morning stew was good. Thick with a stringy meat that tasted to him of rabbit, and accented with a variety of savory leaves and lemony grasses. It was cook food, not food for slaves.

He ate every bit of it, relishing the hints of what he thought of as rosemary and marjoram along with strong dashes of sage. *The scent of bliss*, he thought, and this scent carried his thoughts from Cyvair to Voethe.

When he finished eating, Tandy was not in sight, but he could hear her strong voice carrying from a far corner of the massive kitchen as she chided one of the cooks. For an instant, he saw his mother in her stead, commanding the staff in his father's kitchen, in his father's house.

A long time ago, yet the pain was still there. Tandy seemed old enough to be his mother, but her interest in him was not motherly. She had made that much plain at every opportunity.

He resisted her advances, though not because he found her unattractive. Quite the contrary, she was very attractive if one could look past the protruding eyes that were entirely pupil and iris—and that was easily done. Her yellow skin and the long, lustrous hair-like fur on her thorax reminded him of the exotic, dark-haired beauties of Yug. The smell of her was that of a goddess-created flower. The shape of her was nearly that of a woman in full bloom.

He closed his eyes, sucked in a breath, released. When he opened his eyes, Tandy was standing before him, asking "Good, yah?"

Martin smiled, replied in broken Cikathian. "Yah, good. The best."

Tandy smiled, said something he did not understand. Martin shrugged, began to turn away. Tandy touched her hand to his. "Varthen quarter has many guests today. Full," she said. "They've been arriving since the small hours."

Martin jumped up from the table. "And you feed me when there's—"

"Full bellies make for good work, good thinking," she said, and then she kissed his cheek.

Martin's anger fell away. His smile returned. He could not be angry with Tandy. She was sweet on him, and he could not in all honesty say that he was not sweet on her. He touched a hand to her cheek, started to turn away.

Tandy passed him a satchel of baked and dried goods. He took up the satchel with a quick smile.

—

Sixth toll found Martin in Wuntrus quarter. He had just found another book for Tandy's collection, and it was in the breast pocket of his jacket. He stared at the spear blocking his path with a mixture of fear and annoyance.

The fear was quite rational. The sharp end of the weapon was poised less than a hand from his throat and the Trykathian holding the shaft was large, armored, and fierce-looking. His leaf-green eyes reminded Martin of the boundless depths of a great forest. It seemed to him that if this Trykathian killed him, he would step over Martin's body, regain his post, and forget that Martin ever lived.

That he should be annoyed was also entirely rational, he supposed. He was running late and in a hurry to catch up with the day's tasks. He did not need his way to be impeded and yet it was, and there seemed nothing he could do about it. His mind raced in a hundred different directions, looking for solutions, but none of them were satisfactory.

This was unusual. Normally Martin was on time and on task. He could talk or charm his way around any obstacle. The fact that this Trykathian continued to ignore him was exasperating, but in truth his exasperation had less to do with the Trykathian and more to do with Yarr. Turnings before, he had planned everything, put everything in place. He had been meticulous, but Yarr had made a mess of it all. His failure haunted him ever since, the worse because he had never foreseen it.

This morning he had awoken with a glimmer of how to set everything right. His plans within plans could work, but now less than a toll into this day there already was another complication.

He reached into his satchel, felt for the coarse meat stuffs Trykathians favored. "Little left, but saved for you," he told the other in broken Trykath.

The hard eyes narrowed. "Open it."

Martin glanced at the satchel. "For others," he implored. "You won't like any of it."

"Open it."

Martin took a step away from the spear and complied, opening the satchel to reveal its contents. The green fruits were a favorite of Gnogs. The orange fruits were for Kingdomers. The black bread was for Erlanders. The silver fish were for Alvs. The spicewood was for the Dwelmish. The dark meat was for Trykathians—but what remained was for other Trykathians, not this Trykathian.

The Trykathian put the spear back to Martin's throat. Martin emptied the contents of the satchel onto the stone floor, made a show of revealing that his pockets were empty.

The Trykathian watched with little expression. "You may go away now," he said at last.

"No," Martin replied, "I cannot. I must enter." He tried to stand taller, to make the most of his average height and build. He knew there was little intimidating about his dark hair, hazel eyes, and boyish face, but he could at least be dignified.

The Trykathian grunted, said something too quickly for Martin to understand. Three other Trykathians appeared. They fumbled about, picking up the things Martin had spilled on the stone floor, their large hands and thick fingers making the task difficult.

The first Trykathian regarded Martin. "What are you?"

Martin raised an eyebrow, seeing for the first time the one blocking his path was not the one he usually encountered in the Wuntrus. He cursed himself silently for not seeing this sooner, but it was difficult to tell Trykaths apart. They were all built like tree trunks with little neck to separate their heads from their shoulders. They all had the same square face and flat nose. He switched to Cikathian, as the bounds of his Trykathian had been sorely tested. "I am Day Master of Hearth."

"And you bribe noble protectors?"

"It was but a gift," Martin said. His thoughts turned on the word noble. The phrasing could have been a mistake in his understanding, but somehow he didn't think so. Somehow it was important.

"What does Master of Hearth do?"

"He cares after the fires. Cook fires. Gallery hearths. Foundry furnaces. Chamber fireplaces."

"I see. How does he do this with fruits and breads and meats?"

"Well, he does not. He—"

"Make fire for me," the Trykathian interrupted.

"What?"

"You heard me."

Martin scowled, his exasperation growing. He looked around, hoping to find the one who held his satchel. He did, moved to take it back, but was stopped at spear point.

"My bag, please," Martin said firmly, angry for letting himself get into this predicament. Why hadn't he seen that the Trykathian wasn't the one he usually met? Why hadn't he seen that the heretofore empty chamber was occupied?

The likely answer to that lay in the problem he had been puzzling over. When he worked out things in his head, the rest of the world did not matter.

He picked up the satchel as one of the Trykathian's tossed it down. Its contents spilled, but not badly, and it only took a few heartbeats to gather up everything.

"That's not right," he told himself. In remembrance, he saw the satchel goods spread out on the floor. The fruits separate from the breads and the fish. The spicewood layered within it all.

"Can you or can't you make fire?" the Trykathian challenged.

"Don't interrupt me," Martin said absently, closing his eyes. Yes, there it was, though he had lost the meaning of it.

He stared into it, saw the seeming randomness of it, but there was also order within it. The Gnogs. The Kingdomers. The Erlanders. The Alvs. The Dwelmish. The Trykathians. Like the satchel goods themselves, each had their place. Each had their purpose. They were as instruments, as things to be played. The masters played upon them. He played upon them.

Still something did not fit. Something was not right. Something was missing.

He stared blankly ahead. In his mind's eye, he added other peoples he had heard of and seen but had little dealings with. The Wërg. The Dwëorg. Others.

"Enough!" shouted the Trykathian. "Whatever it is you do, stop! I see no fire!"

Spear or no. Monstrous size or no. Martin glared at the other. He was about to speak, about to be impaled, when he felt a presence like a soft feather tracing the back of his thoughts. The Trykathians took to the ready stance at the same time he prostrated himself.

He did not dare look up. He caught snatches of the rumble-pitched ftokish, sure the speaker was no other than the great master himself. His visit was an honor, a grace, a blessing.

Then he knew he had it. The missing pieces to make it all fit. The Drakón. The titans. The Jurin.

He waited. The voices and the presence faded. He drew himself up. "I am Day Master of Hearth," he said. He noticed distantly that his voice was no longer unsteady. "I will be delayed no longer. I must see to the master's fires."

The Trykathian smiled. On the brutish face, the gesture seemed not only unusual but unnatural. "Not today, perhaps never again."

Martin blinked. "What do you mean?"

The Trykathian pointed to a scrap of vellum near Martin's feet. "Our master is generous."

"It is nothing. I must resume my duties. I must see to the fires." Again, a smile. Martin wondered if a Trykathian smile was like Jurin laughter.

"It is more than nothing. Hand it to me."

Wondering why the Trykathian should care, Martin nevertheless handed the vellum over. The Trykathian examined it briefly, traced the outline of the mark burnt into the vellum. A look bordering on awe crossed his face. He handed the vellum scrap back to Martin.

Martin turned on his heel, turned back. "What is it?" he asked, gesturing at the mark.

"It's his mark."

"Yes, I can see that. For what purpose?"

"Your deliverance."

"My deliverance?"

"Auy, your deliverance." The Trykathian extended his right hand in a fist, palm down, thumb extended inward. Martin glanced to the other Trykathians, saw the gesture for what it was, extended his own hand in a fist. "I am Gerhold of Stone Mountains. These are Kertoth, Fielk, and Marktid. They are also Stone Mountains."

Martin stood awkwardly for a moment, nodded. "I am Martin of Voethe."

Fielk said, "Does it fill you with joy?"

"How so?" Martin asked.

Fielk laughed and the others joined him. Gerhold said, "Fielk means to say, does it bring you happiness?"

Martin decided to admit he had no idea what was going on. "I speak little Trykathian, passable Cikathian. I don't understand any of this."

"What's to understand?" Gerhold said. "You've the mark. Your life is changed."

"It could be this mark was at your feet," Martin said, thrusting the vellum back into the other's hands. "I've no need of a life changed." Outwardly he was calm, but inside his thoughts were in turmoil. *The plan,* he told himself. *The pattern within the pattern.* He could see it now, and nothing else mattered.

"We Stones are already marked. No doubt you wonder about your fire, yet you've no need. Me, Gerhold, I will help you."

"The fire," Martin protested. "I must set the master's fire."

"Not anymore," Gerhold replied. "See…" The Trykathians stepped aside, opening the view. Inside the chamber, the fire in the great hearth was coming to life. "I will take you to the Sorter. She will help you understand, and perhaps she will even reward my efforts."

"It would be a kindness…" Martin began, and then the crush of the world was upon him. Fleetingly, he thought of Tandy and the new book he had for her. Tandy alone had shown him kindness where no others had. Then he thought of Yarr and knew his words were false.

Gerhold chuckled softly. "Ah, so you know something of what comes. You are worried, but need not be. At the least, he honors your service. Perhaps you'll be right in the thick of things when the war comes to the gates."

"War? War with whom?"

Seventh toll sounded. Gerhold looked Martin over. "For now, the Jurins. Perhaps others soon. My offer of help stands. The time of my post has come and gone. Marktid?"

Marktid came to attention, turned about. He took Gerhold's spear, and then stood where Gerhold had been standing. Gerhold looked to Martin.

Martin signaled his agreement, waited. Gerhold pointed out the way. Martin followed.

CHAPTER EIGHTEEN

"Gods be damned," Arger cried out as he fought to hold in his guts with both hands. "Aegot has forsaken me."

Yarr stood behind Arger, surveying the carnage. Side tunnels opened to admit hawkers and gravers. The hawkers cleared the great stage of the corpses; the gravers helped the dying to their end.

Though there were no more foes on the field, Yarr remained wary. His face, chest, and arms were bloody, but it was the blood of others and not his own. The long, spiked chain he gripped and wrapped around his left hand and forearm held the eviscerated flesh of several beasts. He drove the bloody sword he carried in his right hand into the dirt at his feet. "You still draw breath," he told Arger. "Be glad of that."

With the din of battle and cries of the dying gone, he heard the mob in the stands now. Purposefully, his view was to the south. The trisuns of Cyvair were to his back, high overhead. He took in careful breaths as he surveyed death and awaited the judgment. He turned his angry, sullen eyes to the stands, lifted his arms in sign of triumph, but no longer saw any of it. Instead he heard his father's voice in his ears, telling him of the flat, open grasslands and the forests of his beloved Élvemere, and then he saw them, his mother and father, holding hands and standing side by side outside the pavilion of rich blue silks and yellow satins.

"Join us," his father said.

"Yes, join us," his mother said, "Many of your favorites for this repast."

Yarr put haste to his step. "Have you spoken with the ancient ones, mother?"

"I have," the queen said. "I'll tell you all." She took his hand and led him into the pavilion. His father followed a step behind.

Yarr seated his mother at the long table of living oak that bent to his mother's will, and then sat across from her. His father took the seat of honor at the head of the table. The table was overflowing with the fruit of the land and, just as his mother had said, many were his favorites.

His mother poured a full cup of the hot juice of the blue elder and set it before him. "You are angry," she said, "This will soothe and calm."

He drank from the cup. His mother put a plate of anise fern, licorice root, and the fruit of the sweet chervil before him. "This will help you see more clearly."

He ate and waited. "Mother, did they agree?" he asked finally. "Will Shodjen and the other great houses oppose?"

"Just like the young ones," the queen said. "You never did care much for the long talk. Too many formalities and requisites for you. Yet a capacity for waiting is necessary in all things, and especially for working with those who speak with the forest's voice. Learn this and perhaps your father and I can take the Long Walk."

"But I've a need," Yarr said, "I've agreed to every condition."

"Indeed, and now you must understand as I understand. This place between places—" and as his mother said this, she swept her hand in a wide circle, "—cannot be forever. The Light of Élvemere dims and it is our people who maintain what remains. It is time. You must prepare yourself to become the Light of Élvemere, and then this place need be no more."

Death and darkness seemed to be his mother's constant companions of late. Yarr pushed the dark mood aside, focused. "Is this what the ancient ones told you, mother?"

"It is, by leaf and root, and all agreed. It is time."

"Time? Can it be so already?" Yarr asked, looking to his father, but the king's thoughts were elsewhere. "What of the young ones? Surely, they did not agree."

"The ancients spoke with one voice, old and young alike. Even Traflekar while he sung your praises."

Memories of Traflekar swept over Yarr. Traflekar was one of the young ancients, a powerful oak, who had taken Yarr on many an adventure once he had been coaxed from his long slumber. He had introduced Yarr to the Fhur, the Spiraren, and the Entspiraren, had played games with Yarr in the forests and in the places between places. "Traflekar? Has he wed Ityeneria? Has he recovered? Is he well?"

"As well as can be said of a tree," said a voice that boomed and echoed throughout the pavilion, as the living oak that they sat before transformed from table to ent. The familiar face emerging from the wood was Traflekar's, and his pleasure at seeing Yarr's surprise was clear. "Lit-t-t-le Túr-r-ring," the ent said, trilling his t's and rolling his r's as most of the older ents did.

"Traflekar!" Yarr exclaimed, feeling suddenly the boy he had been when he'd last seen the ent. "It is you, and you look well! You will do this thing I've asked. Won't you?"

"I will, Little Túrring," the great oak said solemnly, "and as for Ityeneria, I have begun, but the process is not an easy one. I've still some years of the proposal and some years of her response to manage before talk of marriage can begin. If she'll have me, that is."

"She'll have you," the queen said, "But to the point, now. Let talk stray and we'll all be old before we get back to task, especially when we moot among ents."

"You moot among ent," Traflekar said, a hint of the forest's song in his voice. "This ent has already agreed to help preserve what needs be preserved. All will be set in motion for when it is time."

"What of House Steorra?" Yarr asked.

"The Sons of Jfe side with the Sons of Áthon," his father replied.

"What of the gatehouse?"

The queen sighed, took a long taste of her tea. "The stones and pieces, yes, but it is not built nor can we allow it to be. They've yet to find the one who can build it, but the ancients say they are close, that the search for the builder ends."

"The time approaches," the ent said.

Sudden tears in his mother's eyes spoke of her deep anguish over all that was coming, and though Yarr looked away it did not keep this dark feeling away. For a time after, silence held, and then King Enáthon Túrring said, "Windrunner has sired, a pairing of foals this time. One for you and one for your queen, I should think."

"Dierá, father, have you spoken with her?"

His father did not answer. Instead, his mother said, "Akharran, the great queen. She has birthed too. Strong sons."

The unexpected words caused Yarr to retreat from his second self, and so it was that he returned to his first self awaiting the judgment in the colosseum. The roar of the crowd renewed as he turned about on his heel and faced the box seats for the honored guests and the noble few.

He stood statue still, his arms raised, his voiceless expression mirroring all the bloody rage he felt. The ageless king, Zephyres, and his consort, Makhatar, studied him. To the right of Makhatar, in a place of honor, sat the son of Rnothen, the titan who had come to see his death. The disappointment in the titan's expression was evident, and this disappointment gave Yarr hope that there was meaning in all things. He had no true power. He was as nothing to them, but his win this day was the titan's loss. He was as certain of this as he was of no other thing.

Makhatar gave first sign, pointing at the dirt. The crowd roared approval of her condemnation even as Yarr turned back and swept up the sword from the dirt. Arger, for his part, surely had no clue of what was coming.

Yarr waited, sword and chain in hand. Now it was the ageless king's turn to pass judgment, but he was distracted by something the titan was saying. Yarr had decided long ago that he loathed titans as much as he loathed ageless. Still, it was a special loathing that he held for this one, and this loathing burned in him as brightly as the trisuns burned in the sky above.

He planned the sweep of the blade that would bring Arger's end. The swifter and cleaner the blow, the quicker and less painful the end. He felt sorrow and remorse in those last moments. He had never promised the other he would live to see the next day. He had given hope, though, and hope snatched away was twice bitter.

The titan stood, and so Yarr knew that the king had given away the honor of final judgment. He extended his arm. The crowd quieted. If the titan raised his hand to the heavens, judgment would end at odds—one against and one in favor—so the king would still get a final say. Otherwise, judgment would pass and Yarr must then do his work.

Yarr took a breath, held it. The onlookers, growing impatient, began to shift in their seats. Some called for death; others, life.

The king quieted all by standing. He turned to the titan, and death won out as the titan pointed to the dirt.

"Be strong, Erlander," Yarr said as he swept the blade around and severed Arger's head from his shoulders. "Aegot knows you now."

CHAPTER NINETEEN

Dierá turned her back to the railing. The red silk of her gossamer dress ruffled in the wind. Behind her the world was shrouded in darkness, as was much of the vast palace itself beyond the great glass doors leading away from the balcony.

She listened to the young luvens finish the fourth and final movement of Wettilk's *Resplendent Pursuit*. The resonant notes soaring from glass and wood told of an Alvish king who searched the across time and distance for the one who would become his queen, of how he used a song contest to bring her to him, of how he won her heart with his own composition, and of how he lost her to an unexpected storm.

The melody lingered long after the final notes. Racing within her, it was ecstasy; it helped her transcend. Her soaring heart was all she knew for long moments. Eruption followed; release followed. The grandest release. She floated beyond; became one with all things. She saw the Élvemere that could be once more. She saw her people. She saw him—the one who would become the king of kings:

Rastín. Rastín was not alone. She saw G'rkyr; it was G'rkyr she made love to. She loved him. She loved them both. But it was G'rkyr she chose.

Reverie gave way to reality. The wind on her face she felt first. G'rkyr's hand steadying her she felt next. "They return," he told her.

Dierá turned to the railing. The silk of her dress carried on the wind. In front of her, the shrouded world was still. She took three long breaths, steeled herself inside; becoming ice and fire, for that was what they were together. She was ice; G'rkyr, fire. Upon her signal, the Keeper of the House ushered in a squad of Fedwëorgs clad in house regalia. In the midst of the Fedwëorgs was a chained Drakón of a nation she had only recently come to know.

G'rkyr took up the chains. Dierá dismissed Nostik, the young luvens, and the Fedwëorgs with a wave of her hand. She commanded silence with no more than a look until the balcony emptied.

"My endowments," the Drakón shrieked, "Return them to me!"

"Or what?" Dierá countered as G'rkyr applied his might to the immobilizing chains. This Drakón had but a sliver of the bearing of the Praxixian Prince. He was already lost to panic, reacting instead of acting.

"You'll never get the thing you seek. It will be taken from you over and over."

"You know nothing," Dierá scoffed. She studied the Drakón. While most Drakón seemed to be akin to great winged serpents with scales, claws, and horns, these Drakón were different. Their pale blue heads, adorned with bushy crests, lacked true horns. Their long, broad wings sprouted from thickset torsos and their tails were exceptionally short. Their backs were a slatey blue and their underparts were dark green, with a deep blue band across the upper chest.

"I know—I see," the Drakón shrieked as the chains began to suffocate and crush. "You will never be together."

Dierá held up a hand. G'rkyr relaxed his plying of the chains. "We can continue this discussion in shadow or light. Tell me what you see?" Find resolve, she told herself. She focused her will to ensure her scent did not betray her eagerness.

Enveloping herself in G'rkyr's strength, she thrust herself and the Drakón into shadow. The domain she created was an elongated hollow. The silver glow from her gray eyes showed her inner fire.

"You will tell me all," she said. Tired of the games she played with captured Drakón, her voice carried an open threat.

"I will tell you nothing." The Drakón attacked, uncurling his neck and clawing his way down the narrow hollow.

Dierá lost the calm she sought in fire and again became in her mind more Jurin than Alv. "What were yours are mine. I will never return them, and I leave you now. Alive in shadow but dead to all knowing save me. You will beg when I return for you, and you will tell me all I want to know."

The Drakón locked eyes with Dierá, spoke with another's voice. "Tell me the story of the red ktoth. Please. Please."

Dierá fumed, left the Drakón in shadow, and returned to light, telling G'rkyr to bring in the prince. As the prince entered, he made a show of stretching his wings in the open air. Clearly the prince was pleased by Dierá's expression, and that, coupled with the fact that she did not mask the scent of her gratitude, made him bold.

G'rkyr clenched his hands into fists, ready to strike, but Dierá waved him off. Mechanically she compared the prince's short wings meant for easy maneuvering and his huge claws meant for rending to the other. The difference was striking. One was a slayer; the other, a hunter seeker. "All was as you said it would be."

"My gift to you," the prince said.

Dierá reminded herself that Drakón were a breed apart and that they knew only how to rule. Try as she might to weed it out, this need was ever present. The trick was to figure out what exactly the Drakón wanted to master and control in the moment. "You knew I drew from G'rkyr and you wanted me to know greater power. You wanted me to know your power."

"And so you do."

"I do," Dierá said, almost bitterly as she looked to G'rkyr. She said nothing of the fact that G'rkyr's strength could flow and flow or of the fact that a Drakón's strength came in waves.

"Return it now," the Drakón said matter-of-factly. From the way he spoke, Dierá knew it was the one thing he wanted in this moment.

"I think not," she said. "Much easier to cap and bind—yes—but also much easier to attach and trade—" Raw magic raged from her gaping mouth, her eyes, her outstretched fingers, snapping and popping as it enveloped the prince. "—sinews. His for yours. Yours I hold in trust until I choose otherwise."

The prince drank in the imbued essence. "He is not trained of the line. It will devour and destroy him."

"I know." Dierá stared down the prince, almost daring him to continue, but he remained silent. "When we are on Cyvair, remember who holds the lines of your chains. Kill me, kill G'rkyr, kill him that I seek, and you'll never be whole again."

The prince raised his neck, folded in his great wings while lowering his front quarters. It was a show of supplication but it came with a warning. "I do this as much for myself as because you compel me. Never forget that, Athania Dierá Steorra. If I did not wish it, this would not be."

It was a truth, and understanding it gave Dierá hope. "Nostik," she called out. The Keeper of the House entered. "Show Prince Battikh to his rooms."

"Call me Takhbarre," the Drakón said as Nostik led him away. "No need for formalities in this company."

Dierá glared. The knowing tone unnerved her. As it was meant to, she told herself. Two steps forward, one back. He is drakónus; you are Alvish. She stumped her way to the railing, spread her hands across the cool surface as she took in the grand view. The rising suns told of morning's arrival and made bare her form beneath the silk. Feeling G'rkyr's eyes upon her, she spun around. Her rising anger was as strong as any potion or charm could ever be, and she pushed it down to quell his lust.

"Sing for me, Dierá," G'rkyr said, moving to a seated position before her. "Sing for me, as you sang for him."

Dierá prostrated herself before the gargant but she did not sing. Instead, she reversed her body, putting her back to the cool, base stones. She looked up at him from this lowly position, her wide eyes filled with forced intensity. "And then?" she asked. Not waiting for an answer, she added, "Would you have me then?"

G'rkyr's eyes lit with sacred fire. He spoke his next words carefully, using the Alvish language and not the Jurin. "Your words are meant to wound, but I do not let them. What I feel for you is what I feel, and you know it as deeply but refuse it.

"Take this victory. Taste its sweetness, Dierá. All that we've worked for is coming to pass. When we are done, Jurin and Alvs will be free. Cyvair awaits."

Dierá arched her back as she moved to a seated position and then spun around on the floor to face him. "My feelings for you are twice cursed. This thing between us is monstrous. You speak in Alvish because there are no words for such things in Jurin."

G'rkyr enveloped the whole of her body in one of his great hands. "You don't mean it. You love me as I love you."

Dierá stood in his cupped hand, slipped the red dress from her shoulders and let it fall. "Jurin lust and covet. They don't love. They don't know how, so instead they own and command. A trait you share with the ageless."

G'rkyr hid her nakedness by closing his hand around her then masked himself in flame, leaving only the hand that held her outside its grasp. "And yet I do love, and I do because of you. You showed me kindness and I learned to love. I learned in spite of what I am."

"You are a monster; I am a monster. I have seen what our union brings, and it brings darkness. Your love for me will break you and damn you, and then you will damn me and break me. Our son—yes, our son—will divide all Jurin and break the Hundred Worlds even as we make it whole."

"You've dreamt of a son? Was he whole? Was he Jurin or Alv?" G'rkyr asked, his voice cracking with emotion. All flame extinguished, he said, "I would never damn or hurt you, Dierá. You have to know this. Hurting you would bring the thousand, thousands deaths upon me."

"Take Cyvair for me, G'rkyr," she said, her voice steady and strong. "Strike at the Drakón heart. Do this with all the force of the Jurin peoples and we may be able to avert what comes."

"If Drakón have hearts, they do no beat as yours or mine do. Have you not learned that yet? The prince, he will take us through and into the city. It is what you said and it has taken so long to get—"

He broke off as Dierá succumbed suddenly to great fits of sobs. "I've deceived you," she whimpered. "Everything I've told you has been a lie. Follow this path and you *will* die a thousand, thousands deaths. All Jurin will die a thousand, thousand deaths."

"But you said this path brings freedom to the peoples. Jurin and Alvs above all others."

Dierá's cheeks were streaked with hot tears. "This freedom you seek will be your end. In the ages to comes, none will even know Jurin once were."

"But I will be free. You said so, Dierá. I taste freedom now, but I am not free. To know the true taste, I will take on all the gods, sell my soul to D'rk'r the Dark, forsake the Merciless whose namesake I am—"

Dierá stopped him with a withering look and said no more. Instead, she showed him everything, starting with little G'rkyr, and this sight awed him—but in the beyond, the great cities burned. The worlds burned. Dust and ash and fire filled the skies of the Hundred Worlds.

"Lies, lies," G'rkyr shouted. "No one can know what comes for a certainty."

Dierá spun the vision closer and closer. With the drau world wrapped around her, she stepped into the revelation and urged G'rkyr to follow. She stood with her back straight, her head level, even in the face of a raging gale that sought to sweep her from her perch atop the jagged cliffs. To the west, the wide bowl of a valley spread to distant foothills. Beyond the foothills, snow-capped mountains of blue-black rock stood as they had for millennia.

Dierá was certain G'rkyr knew this place. It was Süttak, formal seat of the Three Hammers. The valley was home to Anaste, Eternal City of the Hammer, and Wënoste, Guiding Hand of the Warrior. Both sacred and both burned.

"Lies, lies," he screamed. The rage and pain in his voice caused Dierá to lose her hold on the Path. The vision faded. The world of the present returned.

"Why?" G'rkyr asked. The anguish in his voice as he said that one word gave Dierá hope. Jurin were not beasts. They could feel. She gave herself to him then, and not because he wanted her to but because she wanted to. Pain and joy were two sides of the same coin, as were hate and love.

Later that night, when she spoke to her father in dream, she told him of the hope she felt in her heart. Though she still dared not tell him of G'rkyr or the Jurin, she told him of other things.

"There is hope, father," she said. "He loves me as I love him. I feel it as surely as I feel that I will see Eldri soon."

Her father took her hand and walked with her. "You have done well. Our people will live in your deeds. Élvemere will be once more."

Dierá stopped midstride, turned to regard her father. "I believe because you believe."

CHAPTER TWENTY

Martin and Gerhold traveled in silence. The thick-limbed Gerhold led.

A toll passed. They walked along wide corridors, up stairs, through many turnings and through many doors. The air began to smell sweet, fresh, almost of flowers and grass. Strange smells for the Phatidh but Martin was certain that they were in no other quarter of the city.

He wondered at the other's stamina. He was drenched in sweat and yet Gerhold, who towered over Martin and wore heavy leathers, was dry. Perhaps Trykathians did not sweat like men. Still, it seemed to Martin that Gerhold should share his weariness. The path from the Wuntrus to the Phatidh was a long one by tunnel or by stair and hall.

Martin paused to rest In a secluded courtyard and shared the foodstuffs in his satchel. A loaf of heavy black bread. A smoked silver fish. Gerhold seemed to enjoy both. Handfuls of water from a cascading fountain helped to wash it down.

They came to stand before a doorway guarded by two S'h'dith. The guards, clad in spiked helms and heavy chainmail marked with red, carried spears with long wide blades running halfway down their length and short thrusting swords. Both weapons had blades that were quadrisected and meant for impaling.

Gerhold bunched his brows and looked to Martin. Instinctively, Martin held out the scrap of vellum.

The guards opened the doors, revealing a grand garden the likes of which was new to Martin, for there were no flowers, shrubs, or trees. Instead there were strange rocks jutting up from beds of smaller rocks. Some of the jutting rocks were cut at odd angles; others had a more natural look, almost as it they had grown out of the earth below. They were of all colors and sizes. A few were of such impossible size that they seemed to scrape the outer circle of domes high above. Beneath the central inner dome was a fountain, but it ran with fire and not water.

Martin reached out and gripped Gerhold's arm. He held out the vellum scrap, twisted it so the mark showed clearly.

Gerhold said, "Put that away until asked for."

"You say that you are marked. Are all of the Protectorate marked? Is that what the mark is for?"

"The mark is as it is. It is a good thing," Gerhold said firmly, but the firmness seemed appended as if to reassure himself as much as Martin.

"The Protectorate—"

"—serves."

Gerhold looked suddenly uneasy.

Martin asked, "Is something wrong?"

Gerhold shrugged. "A feeling is all. Likely nothing, but everything seems wrong. Out of place."

"And what is out of place?"

Gerhold pointed up the path that dissected the garden. Martin followed with his eyes, saw a long line of those who held a scrap of vellum. "There's more," he said, pointing to other paths dissecting the garden, each with their own lines.

"Do you know what any of this means?" Martin asked as he studied those in the lines. They seemed to be of all peoples. He saw scaly Gnogs, bug-eyed Begreths, wiry Alvs, stocky Dwelmish, scrawny Erlanders, thick-limbed Trykaths, and raven-haired Kingdomers.

"I thought I did," Gerhold admitted. "But this? This is more. I go now."

Martin got in line behind a rather hairy Dwelm, began to thank Gerhold for his help, but saw that Gerhold was not going anywhere. The great doors behind them closed and no one was there to open them. Suddenly he longed for the solace of his hearth duties, and wished he had told Tandy how he felt about her. He touched the book in his breast pocket and felt a pang in his heart.

Gerhold seemed to have his own regrets, and it was with much apprehension that Martin met the other's iron stare. "I'm a damned fool. The more I think I know the less it seems I actually do."

"To know all is to be a master," Gerhold replied, and the wisdom of that simple phrasing made Martin rethink what he thought he knew about Trykaths.

The line moved slowly forward, toward the center of the garden. Martin's eyes roamed the strange stone plots and the deportment of those in the lines. He talked absently with Gerhold, mostly of things of no consequence. He asked about the Protectorate and about how Gerhold had come to serve. He talked with great warmth of Tandy and her kitchens. He lamented his hearths and bemoaned visits beyond the stone walls.

"All as nothing to one who carries the mark. Marked are no longer things to have or not have. Marked serve."

"Dubious distinction," Martin muttered half to himself as he searched the lines with his eyes, failing to see the difference between slave and servant. If that indeed was the distinction Gerhold was trying to make.

Gerhold quietly said, "Great Mother Beqheth, what have I done?" It was a statement as much as it was a question. The Trykath's concerned eyes and general anxiety told Martin that the other was coming to a decision about something. Martin assumed it was whether to walk away and leave Martin to his own ends, or stay and help even if there were unanticipated consequences.

Martin thumped the book in his pocket, spoke before the other could decide. "No Wërg or Dwëorg. No Jurin. No masters. Only us who serve and toil."

"In that you are wrong," Gerhold said, pointing. Martin stepped around the hulking Trykath, followed the other's gaze. He saw what the other saw and it could be no other than the Great One, Makhatar. The throng that surrounded her seemed to confirm this, as did the S'h'dith warriors clad in golden armor. Gerhold seemed to confirm this too by averting his eyes while praising the glory of the heavens.

Until this day Martin had never seen the ageless king, but now he had seen both Zephyres, King of Kings, and Makhatar, King's Consort. But *seen* was not exactly the right word, and Martin knew it. He had not seen Zephyres. He had not dared look, but as for Makhatar, he found he could not look away.

If it were possible for a Drakón to be beautiful, Makhatar was. She was not like the grave, winged behemoths that were her kin. She was as unlike them as Martin was unlike Gerhold. Her back was a brilliant copper and her underparts were barred with silver and blue, save for a golden band across her upper chest. Her wings were barbed but she had no horns. Her tawny brown head was crowned with a double crest and her great, round eyes had golden irises and jet black pupils. It gave her a somewhat owl-like appearance, but a blunted muzzle with savage jaws spoiled the effect.

Martin started to say something when Gerhold struck him a blow that knocked him to his knees. Martin gasped, started to speak. Gerhold struck him a blow that left him flat. From this position, he found himself in her presence. "The Great One?" Martin asked, the words escaping his lips even as he sought to stop himself.

One and the same, came the voice into his mind. *You are a rare one, Martin of Voethe. I felt your presence the moment you entered the recreatory. You may look up, so that I may know you.*

Gerhold nearly took Martin's head off as Martin started to look up, but Makhatar stopped Gerhold with her eyes. "Protector, blame him not. He could do no other than speak. I compelled it from him. I wanted to know him."

Gerhold kneeled, bowed his head. At her touch, Gerhold nearly lost himself to convulsions and tears. Martin was unsure which would win out until the other succumbed to quiet sobs.

Makhatar motioned for Martin to stand. When he did, he noticed that he and Gerhold were surrounded by Makhatar, her entourage, and her soldiers. She put a clawed index finger under his chin and raised his gaze to hers. *Have you no fear, Martin of Voethe? My gaze, my touch, brings ease and not distress. Why is this?*

Martin dared not speak but he held her gaze. All thoughts save one emptied from his mind and that thought was of her beauty. Makhatar reflected an apportionment of her thoughts to him as she took in his dark hair, hazel eyes, and frail humanness. The one word she passed to him in thought was in regard to his build. *Scrawny.*

"Who are you, Martin of Voethe?" It was a question but not a question. Martin was not expected to answer. He understood this and remained silent.

Makhatar worked in this silence, ripping rivers of thoughts from his mind. Against his will, Martin clasped his hands over his face and cried out in agony. To keep himself, he focused on Tandy and his affection for her, but this only seemed to enrage Makhatar. "Who has taught you this?" she bellowed.

Martin's focus went beyond Tandy to her kitchens. He thought of the kitchen aromas. The sweet smell of baking breads. The savory smell of roasting meats. The pungent herbs hanging from the rafters.

Perhaps this will teach you fear, she told him in thought while saying aloud, "What a seditious thing you are. How subversive your thoughts."

This caused murmurs and gasps. It all seemed like theater, like he was the day's entertainment. He was certain Makhatar spoke of the things he dared not think of. It drove his focus. He imagined himself together with Tandy in the kitchens as it had been that morning, but that line of thought was a mistake.

With a clawed finger and thumb, Makhatar ripped the book from his pocket and dropped it to the ground. He braced himself for what Makhatar must surely deliver, feeling only sorrow for involving Gerhold in such a thing. Gerhold would die, though he was as blameless as any others Martin would be compelled to implicate.

His thoughts went to Yarr, and suddenly Martin was gravely certain Yarr too would die. He cursed himself. He should have burned the book. He should have burned all the books.

His thoughts of Yarr brought a sudden change to Makhatar. She seemed to be seeing Martin for the first time. Her thoughts reflecting back on him showed her standing in a room adorned with living tapestries, and upon each measures of his life played out.

In one, Martin saw himself as a boy of seven taking lessons from his father's sage. It was a sad day, a sad moment in the small hours after his mother's death. The lessons were of the Circle and the Path, of how his mother would live on in his memories.

In another, Martin saw himself as a boy of ten running down a cobbled street as buildings burned around him. It was the Reckoning day. The terror in his eyes was for his father, his brothers and his sisters, and not for himself. After finding his father dead, slaughtered on the steps of the chapel house, he led his brothers and sisters to safety in the mountains.

In one more, Martin saw himself as a boy of twelve leading a small group of other boys. The Jurin camp at the base of the mountains was the objective. Neither he nor any of his companions were what he considered soldiers, so he directed the mission as one of stealth and sabotage. It was the first of many such missions.

There was one of his capture the following summer. One of his descent into bondage. One of his betrayal to the pits. One of his first encounter with Yarr, followed by a steady succession of those showing his interactions with Yarr. These seemed a special focus, more so than his struggles to stay alive in the colosseum, more so than his passage out of the pits, but there was interest in how Yarr had convinced the Trojk Master of Keys to help get Martin into hearth service.

Then suddenly Makhatar said, her voice booming across the garden like thunder in the air, "Death to all." On her command, her soldiers rush out in all directions. Their spears prepared to impale; their swords to rend.

Martin steeled himself, intending to stand his ground. He had known better than to believe a mark made him special. He stepped protectively in front of an irrational and still Gerhold. He dared not speak, but he held Makhatar's gaze.

His stance made Makhatar roar loudly. "Filled with rue and shame," she said as she reached out and picked up Martin.

Knowing his death was imminent, Martin did not hold his tongue. He played the role it seemed Makhatar wanted him to play. "I am subversive and seditious. I deserve death, but let the others live. Gerhold is blameless. Doubtless all are blameless."

"My, you are the one, *aren't* you?" Makhatar waved the soldiers back. "Do you know who I am? What they call me? I am the Sorter. King's Consort. I deal with whispers by finding the whisperers. I sort. I alone decide who lives and who dies. Death when I give it is eternal."

She turned Martin upside down, shook loose the things in his pockets. She looked to the satchel next, ripping it apart and clawing at the foodstuffs it contained.

Careful, lest you cease to amuse and interest. Makhatar told Martin in thought.

Martin ignored her, spoke anyway while she dangled him upside down, unable to keep passion from his voice. "We amuse you. We are your playthings. But you will never truly break us no matter what you make us do."

Makhatar's entourage fell to discord and shouts. "His death will be too good for him." "Skin him." "Roast him." "Death for all."

Now I must appease them. Makhatar whispered to him. She pointed to one of the soldiers, said, "Protector, step forward."

The other stepped forward. Makhatar dropped Martin.

"Your spear, give it to this one." She indicated Martin. Martin refused the spear, but Makhatar, with the barest thrust of her will into his thoughts, compelled him to take it.

From that point on, Martin became little more than her puppet. With her thoughts, she ordered him to ready the weapon. He refused; she compelled it. She ordered him to turn. He refused; she compelled it. She ordered him to run Gerhold through. He fell upon the spear instead, and ran himself through.

Raucous laughter was the last thing Martin expected to hear, but it was what he heard.

"Your death comes when I command it, and not a heartbeat before." Makhatar pulled the spear from his hands, used it to split his stomach and spill his entrails onto the dark stones. She thrust the spear back into his hands. "Kill that one and live."

Martin smiled. Blood trickled out of his mouth, but he made no other move. Discord and disbelief returned. "He is damned." "His death will deliver us." "Free him of his life." "Punishment above all else."

Makhatar silenced all with a swing of her great tail. She looked to Martin, said with ice in her voice, "You and the Soulless One are two halves of the same whole. You are indeed the one. Live now because it is my will."

Martin's entrails curled in on themselves and returned to his chest cavity. The gaping hole in his chest closed and then was no more. The all-consuming pain left last, lingering for many steady beats of his heart as if by Makhatar's will.

Makhatar hooked a clawed finger under his chin, used this hold to lift him into the air. "You have been sorted, Martin of Voethe. From this day forth, unless I command otherwise, you are my executioner, willing or not."

She dropped him. Compelled him to pick up the spear. Compelled him to kill. He ran Gerhold through because her hold on him did not allow him to do otherwise. He attacked her when she released him, swinging the spear but missing. This action brought every blade and claw within reach. They skewered him, ripped him apart limb by limb.

Death did not follow. Makhatar refused it by putting him back together. She brought Gerhold back next. Martin was certain she would make him kill Gerhold again, but she did not. Instead she said, "You have been sorted, Gerhold of the Stone Mountains. From this day forth, unless I command otherwise, you are the executioner's assistant, willing or not."

CHAPTER TWENTY-ONE

"Return soon," Nostik told Dierá. Tears were in the yellow-skinned, bug-eyed luven's eyes. Dierá could not honestly say that she would miss the luven homeworld. In truth, sight of the luvens with their protruding eyes and thick thorax covered in long hair-like fur unsettled her more than that of the worst of the Drakón. She had to steel herself whenever Nostik touched her. But she knew in her heart she would miss Nostik. He was attentive, honest, and loyal, and that was as much as she could ask of anyone under the current circumstances.

On the far side of the expansive platform, Zanük marshaled great 1,000-member columns. Fhurjurin stood alongside Empyrjurin. Styrjurin with Monsjurin and Hylljurin. Notably missing were the sæjurin, as they were allied with the ageless.

G'rkyr watched the columns pass in review. His right hand was balled into a fist and pressed against the apex of his chest. He was clad in the ceremonial battle regalia of his enclave: a massive græsteel helm crowned with steel thorns, spiked armor with golden bands intertwined with blue chains, chain leggings trimmed in spikes and barbs, and græsteel boots of such fine steel weaves that they kissed the feet of the wearer.

Dierá looked on from the floating circle several chains away. Her pink chiffon dress floated on the breeze. She did not begrudge G'rkyr this honor. Regardless of whether G'rkyr ever convinced Nük T'nyr to assault Cyvair openly, the support of the Jurin armies was vital to her plans. The many decisive victories under G'rkyr's command in this remote place meant something to Jurin who esteemed strength, decisiveness, and success above all else. In G'rkyr's absence, Zanük would serve as adjunct commander. The ceremony marked the change of command.

In each column, two Empyrjurin were marked with blue. After passing in review, these members of the columns broke ranks and formed up to G'rkyr's left. These few were Morkurhedwa—a chosen few who had vowed to become a living testament to their appellation. Among Empyrjurin, becoming Morkurhedwa was a great honor.

Members of the twelve and twenty clans contested for the right to become the blessed death. Memories of bloody matches still haunted Dierá's dreams at times, for G'rkyr had not only to contest, but to become a chosen one among the chosen few. The selection distinguished him and gave him back his life for the greater good of the clans. Nük T'nyr himself had come, direct from the Siege of R'hamtil, to congratulate his son. The occasion had been seen by those who served G'rkyr as an honor even greater than the selection as Morkurhedwa Praefect itself.

Nostik's touch on her arm pulled Dierá from her thoughts. The scent of him suddenly was honey sweet. Dierá felt uneasy, almost queasy. She forced herself to focus. She turned her head, saw Nostik as if through a thin veil. The bug-eyed luven was luminous, bathed in a sudden penetrating florescence.

"Be calm," Nostik said. "I've scented you. It will become a part of you now so that other luven forever will see you as I see you. Before your arrival, the Jurin dealt fists. Since your arrival, hands. It matters to me not whether this was because of you or because of your presence. You are a friend, Dierá, and I want all luven to know this. In the face of the cleansing that comes, it is the only gift I can offer for kindness."

Dierá found herself at a loss for words. She praised Nostik as best as she could, given her limited ability to focus. Nostik directed the circle back to the palace grounds and docked on the second level balcony nearest to Dierá's rooms. He led her to a large couch upholstered in golden silk and threaded with what looked like the visages of great birds of prey but was in fact a swarm of luven.

"Sit," he told her. "The effects will wear off soon. This bonding protects as well. No other luven can effervesce you now."

Dierá lounged quietly for nearly a toll. G'rkyr's return aroused her. She helped him remove his armor. The helmet alone looked like it should weigh as much as she but was surprisingly light, as were all the pieces of the ceremonial regalia. Jurin craftsmanship with græsteel was as close as she had ever seen to Alvish with lithsteel.

"It is nearly done," G'rkyr said as Dierá worked around him.

Dierá looked up at him while working free his left boot. "It has only just begun." Her tone made it seem a scolding, but she had meant it to come out otherwise. She had meant it to be a show of strength. A show of her resolve.

"A hundred Morkurhedwa would break this world if asked. If asked they would strike Cyvair though all the armies of the Hundred Worlds would fall upon them."

"I did not question resolve—" Dierá started to say, but she did not want to argue. She decided to pleasure him instead. Today was a day of celebration; she wanted it to be joyous. One way sealed it. When he finished, she helped him dress, choosing a shirt and half pants, both of heavy cloth lined with thick fur.

A short walk to the greeting hall followed. Their movements at times like these were a careful dance. Five of Dierá's small steps to one of G'rkyr's great ones. Her haste to his saunter.

Zanük entered unannounced a few tocks later. He was clad informally in blue and yellow cloths. The look was a stark contrast to the official uniforms Dierá always had seen him in before. She guessed the clothes marked something she did not understand.

"Brother," Zanük and G'rkyr shouted at nearly the same time. The two embraced as only Jurin could, smashing heads, locking arms around backs and lifting first one and then the other off his feet. Dierá, as ever, imagined two mammoth bears coming together, locking paws and jaws. Both were in high spirits. The command transfer had gone smoothly without the usual grumblings and opposition.

Jdes, the enclave's Scarabaeid Praefect, entered next. Jdes was the right hand of Kurl'k. He saw with Nük T'nyr's eyes. Anything he saw or knew, Nük T'nyr saw and knew.

Dierá quietly moved several steps back and to G'rkyr's left so she was hidden partially behind G'rkyr and almost out of view. The position was one of highest deference. Alvs were a people conquered by Jurin. The conquered served or were unseen. She had no formal function at this moment, and so she must be unseen. It would not always be so, and she knew this.

"They honor you," Jdes said loudly. Dierá did not know what the other was talking about until G'rkyr, Zanük, and Jdes moved to the far end of the hall and Jdes opened the great windows. Dierá knew then that it was a blooding from the sounds of wailing and the pungent smell of burning flesh, ash, and copper.

Jdes clasped G'rkyr's shoulder on one side and Zanük's on the other. "We feast," he said as he crashed himself and the other two through the windows and rode a bridge of power with them to the platform below.

Dierá ran from the room, frantic. She rushed first to Nostik's quarters. Finding his room empty, she hurried to the servant's wing. She need not have hurried. All the rooms were empty, even those for the youngest luven. She saw their faces; heard their lyrical music. Her heart bled. In one of the windows that faced west by northwest, she saw them then, the great piles of the burning. She had kept this reality as far from her thoughts as possible.

G'rkyr had told her once that armies marched on their stomachs as much as on their boots. She had known the luven had many purposes. Their moderate intellect and easy mannerisms made them good servants if poor soldiers. Their hive mentality and ability to breed swarms made them good food sources if at times too abundant.

She walked at a sedated pace back to her rooms, crawled onto the couch of golden threads and cried herself to sleep. She did not dream, but she did awake to something unexpected. It was Takhbarre, who came of his own volition. How long he watched her she did not know, but she did know that in however long it was he could have killed her and had chosen not to. There were no servants to announce or track his comings and goings. Jurin and all others were occupied elsewhere in feasting and festivities.

Takhbarre said, "Only Empyrjurin feast like that before conflict. It supposes triumph before that triumph is earned."

Dierá assumed the barb was for her benefit, but its hearing did not please her. She wiped the wetness from her cheeks as she sat up. She focused herself on Élvemere and the rebirth of her people, became again a queen of queens. "You could have taken your freedom just now."

Takhbarre made a soft mournful sound. "Athania Dierá Steorra, you think you are at your best when you take on regal airs yet it is quite the opposite. To be the thing you want to be you must cast back the walls."

"I think I've opened myself to you quite enough," Dierá said. "You are not my ally, so don't pretend to play the part of one."

"Likely you'll never know what part I play," Takhbarre said half to himself. "I'm not here as outlet to your pain. Rather, to tell you of new whispers. It is time. You must begin."

"And I'm to—"

"In The Abundance, there is discord. To wait until the morning would be too late."

"And I should what? Interrupt the festivities of G'rkyr, Zanük, Jdes, and the whole of the Morkurhedwa?"

He said aloud, "A queen of queens would," while whispering to her in thought. *Isn't that the thing you most want to be?*

Dierá fled the sitting room, going to her bedchamber and closing the double doors behind her. Her haste was not because she trusted the Prince of Praxix, but rather because she could not be certain he was not telling the truth. Perhaps he had looked into the Path and seen their victory. Just as easily, though, he could have seen their defeat. Either way, a decision was needed.

She changed out of her finery and into the servant's garb that was laid out for the morning. The two gold armbands she slipped up her right arm to her bicep told of her service in an important house. The red armband that followed told that she was the head of that household service. The final black armband gave her free passage in the slaveways and limited passage beyond.

G'rkyr's garb as personal champion and protector was more tenuous. Few Drakón kept Jurin servants even before the Hundred Worlds War began. Fewer still did now, primarily only those who served in posts where Jurin assaults were common. Dierá did not fully understand the reasoning behind it, but it was what it was. More important was the fact that Praxix was not one of those posts. Takhbarre had never before kept Jurin.

In choosing the guises, Dierá had asked the prince many pointed questions. All the answers pointed to the choices she had made. There was no time now for second guesses. Action was needed. She swept up G'rkyr's things, rushed from the room.

The halls were empty. She took the grand stairs, raced outside to the review platform.

She hurried past the dwindling piles of roast luven. She was disgusted, but resolved. Her focus was on what she must do.

G'rkyr, Zanük, and Jdes were inside one of the hastily erected pavilions feasting and drinking. Empyrjurin did not drink strong spirits before battle; they left that vice to those they conquered. Their drink was watered and mostly of a fiery substance that helped their eum flow. Eum was the wellspring of their power. It gave them fire and strength.

Dierá bowed and kneeled when she came to stand before G'rkyr. She did not speak, nor did she look at him. Instead, she held out the clothes as if to remind him that it was time. She meant the gesture as one to steal him away quietly. G'rkyr, not one to understand subtlety truly, stood abruptly, upsetting the table and knocking over his chair in the process.

Eyes that had not seen Dierá's entrance now did. It was Zanük who came to her aid, sweeping her up and pulling G'rkyr away before Jdes could say anything. Outside beyond the pavilions and fires, Zanük set Dierá down. G'rkyr spoke first. "The luven," he said, "I know it upsets you. The razing is custom. None now can speak our secrets. I told you of the luven's purpose. The hive will be reborn. It is the way, and even Nostik will be Nostik once more, though he will not know all things of this life."

G'rkyr's words were as close to apology as his nature allowed. Dierá looked beyond Zanük and G'rkyr and saw plenty who could give away secrets. She started to throw her anger at him, thought better of it. She had not come to argue. "That Praxin says we must go now. That morning will be too late."

Both Zanük and G'rkyr knew Dierá referred to Takhbarre. It was understood. She did not say his name because of the perceived power it gave him. Zanük and G'rkyr asked the same question at the same time, "You trust him in this?"

Dierá could not honestly say that she did, but waiting until morning seemed more wrong than acting now. "I trust only that we must do something now. Either he has seen our destruction or our salvation. Moving now seems to be the right choice. Waiting seems more wrong."

"We move," G'rkyr said without hesitation, raising a fist to show his resolve.

Zanük showed that he concurred by raising a fist to his brother's. Within a half toll, the Morkurhedwa were formed up and waiting. They were one hundred strong, dressed in black steel and blue helms. Dierá stood beside Takhbarre. Zanük and G'rkyr said wordless goodbyes, clasping shoulders and thumping fists. Jdes opened a way portal for them, pulling the power from the earth at their feet and wrapping it with precision until the way opened.

The Morkurhedwa poured into the gate, fought their way out the other side, and then secured the area as needed. G'rkyr, Dierá, and Takhbarre followed. Jdes was last. He rode the final weaving of power out of the gate as the way closed behind them.

The first transition point was Ferfothin, a Trykathian world. G'rkyr expected little resistance. It seemed to Dierá that was what the Morkurhedwa found. Six transitions remained.

CHAPTER TWENTY-TWO

Dierá bled and defended. It seemed the closer they got to the Drakón homeworld, the more resistance they encountered. This was not how it was supposed to have been. The way was supposed to take them through remote places and not into populated zones. She did not understand why they exited the gates in increasingly populated zones.

To her it seemed that either Jdes was incompetent or they were compromised. G'rkyr assured her otherwise as he defended himself with a two-handed stroke of his græsteel blade. "Five transitions on a direct line for Cevis al'Der, where my father's armies begin their strike."

It was not the plan she had agreed to previously. If true, why was she fighting for her life and bleeding on the purple rocks of Megris Dahwan? Where were the Morkurhedwa? Where was Takhbarre?

Jdes arched lightning directly at her. She dodged it but her attacker did not. The blue-white bolt caught the sæjurin full in the chest. He collapsed in agony at her feet.

With one long sweep of his blade, G'rkyr gutted his foes, a trio of Gnog pikers clad in a peculiar honey and rose colored armor. G'rkyr, Dierá, and Jdes regrouped and ensured there were no more foes. "My father's armies strike while we move on. Two transitions on a tangent to Cyvair."

"That was not the plan," Dierá countered.

"It is as much of any plan as any Alv should know," Jdes said.

His voice reminded Dierá of her place. She took three steps back and to the right, putting G'rkyr between herself and Jdes. In G'rkyr's shadow she healed herself, thankful the blood had not soiled her clothes.

She squatted down, took in deep breaths. It had been a long time since she defended with a weapon other than words. She had almost forgotten the feel of steel in her hands and the taste of blood on her lips. The early days after Karthold had been all steel and blood. She had earned G'rkyr's esteem with the same.

In the daypack at her side, Dierá found a clean cloth. She wet it using her waterbag; used it to clean herself. She washed G'rkyr next, removing the muck, blood, and guts from his arms, face, and neck while he cleansed his blade using a whetstone and fire. Jdes mocked her when she turned to him next. His scorn-filled laughter was abridged as much by G'rkyr's cutting stare as by her healing touch to a deep cut in his arm.

Dierá did not expect gratitude. Her act was not one of kindness or of need. It was one of pretense. Normally an Empyrjurin would have sealed such a wound with fire and taken the scar as a tribute to a contest won. Her purpose was to be seen. If plans had changed, she wanted Jdes to know her uses. She had proven herself apt in combat, purposefully taking on sæjurin over Gnogs; now she proved herself apt in wolskill. Jurin knew little of the healing crafts so she hoped the statement she made was clear.

Finished, she returned to her place in G'rkyr's shadow. She felt Takhbarre's absence as keenly as she felt the absence of the Morkurhedwa. Silently she battled her misgivings. She had misjudged G'rkyr; never credited his intellect or his ability to deceive. Were other betrayals ahead? Or had he simply put his people's needs first as she would soon?

—

Martin stood beside Gerhold in stunned silence. Makhatar gave him Gerhold's leash as if the other was a prize. Martin took the leash; he had no other choice. Any act that he did not perform of his own volition, Makhatar compelled him to do.

Constant struggle against the compelling was draining. Martin lost track of time. It had been some days since the sorting, but he knew not the exact count. The first execution had been the hardest. He had not expected it to occur in the colosseum but it had. Makhatar passed judgment and he as her executioner delivered it. It was a new twist to the games and the gathered throng reveled in it.

Each day brought something new. He was beginning to understand the microcosm of Makhatar's entourage. They were of many peoples, including titan and Drakón, but not Jurin or Gnog. At first glance they seemed to be free to come and go as they chose. In truth, not a one was truly free, and they might as well have worn the same leashed collars that he and Gerhold wore.

The pecking order was defined mostly by rank and race. Drakón and titans were at the top, followed by S'h'dith. For the most part, these seemed to be royals of some sort or another, even among S'h'dith. Martin had not known that the snake people served any purpose other than as warriors and magi. He wondered if S'h'dith were newly elevated as Jurin once had been.

A Wërg, a Fedwëorg, and a Fhurtroll at the next rung were oddities, but also particularly valued prizes. The fourth rung, and the one he aspired to, included Alvs and Dwëorgs. He was the only Kingdomer, and the others lamented this greatly. His frailty was their doom. He would die a ghastly death if any of them forgot themselves for a moment, and then they would never hear the end of it. He guessed then that what Makhatar had said about him dying only when she wished it was more likely to be whenever she became bored with him, or allowed his death because of benign neglect.

The Drakón and titans had their own pets. These mostly were Trykathians, as they were considered heartier than Kingdomers and Goeks. There was some sort of odd power struggle between Gerhold and these Trykathians. Martin did not understand it, and was too busy trying to figure out the new rules to pay particular attention. Understanding the dynamics of the group and their rules was the key to carving out his place within it.

Moving the gaggle that was the entourage was a logistical nightmare. Makhatar did not care how the feat was accomplished, but when she looked for the entourage it must be present and formed exactly as she expected it to be. If she had a certain type of witty or sarcastic comment, her closest titan was expected to be at hand. His expected response was a haughty cackle and a compliment to her wit. If she was being petty and vile, her Drakón had best be close. They were expected to echo her acrimony. For other moments, her favored pets—the Wërg, Fedwëorg, and Fhurtroll—must jostle for her eye. It was all a grand theater; its purpose seemed to be to keep Makhatar and her inner circle from boredom.

Makhatar did not take Martin everywhere with her. At times, he and Gerhold spent many long tolls in the dark rooms where lesser members of the entourage slept at night. The rooms were several floors removed from Makhatar's own rooms. At these times Martin hoped Makhatar had become bored with him and forgotten about him, yet this thought also caused him great distress.

He and Gerhold had no way to leave the dark rooms. If Makhatar should go off world or beyond the city and forget about those in her rooms, they would all starve and die. Only at Makhatar's request did the doors open. Only in Makhatar's presence was there food, drink, and light. It was as if they existed only when she said they existed.

This day, however, was different. Makhatar kept him close from the day's earliest light. He knew not why, but the chatter was all about the coming entertainment. The expected spectacle was all anyone could talk about.

—

Jdes prepared a gate. Threaded magics began their spiral, opening the way. G'rkyr prepared to enter. Dierá walked behind him. She was certain all was lost.

Moments before they stepped away the miraculous happened. The Morkurhedwa returned with Takhbarre. He was bound and chained, which seemed to please Jdes more than the sight of the Morkurhedwa. Dierá knew then that his hatred of Drakón was even keener than hers. Useful information.

"Cevis al'Der was not part of the agreement," Takhbarre shrieked.

G'rkyr struck Takhbarre and scoffed. "You were given a choice."

"I'm Prince of Praxix," Takhbarre replied. "I'll not proceed until our terms are clear."

G'rkyr indicated to the Morkurhedwa that they should remove the chains, and they did. Takhbarre was pushed through the gate against his will. G'rkyr and Dierá went next. Jdes pulled himself through on the final weaving of power.

They emerged not on a world or moon, but in a nexus. Much like Dierá's shadow-created hollows, this place existed outside of the ordinary world. It was a place between places; it connected paths of several gate clusters. Arrival here gave Dierá a glimpse of how Jdes opened gates so easily. It made his aura as radiant as a star, and the dull tracings between him and the Morkurhedwa visible. Her lesser aura and lesser tethers to G'rkyr and Takhbarre were visible as well, but masked by his far greater luminosity.

She was careful to keep to the shadows behind G'rkyr and Takhbarre. Jdes did not need to know her inner strength.

Takhbarre continued his protestations even as Jdes showed G'rkyr the way out. The Morkurhedwa exited with G'rkyr, Takhbarre, and Dierá. Jdes did not. He kept the exit open until the Morkurhedwa had secured the exit point and returned, closing the gate and leaving G'rkyr, Takhbarre, and Dierá alone in a dark tunnel.

G'rkyr did not need to speak the word on his lips for Dierá to know this was Cyvair. Takhbarre had already told her this by his demeanor. The Drakón seemed to know immediately, either by scent or sense. It also could have been his brief embrace of The Abundance. Dierá felt him reach out to it, but she thought she blocked him before he touched it. For long moments afterward, his complaints stopped and his eyes never left Dierá's.

"You want this thing," he told her. "I no longer trust them, but I trust you. Give me your word on what we agreed to and that you had no part—"

"—My word," Dierá said. G'rkyr started to say something; she cut him off with an icy stare. "That was between G'rkyr and his. I am as betrayed as you."

"Then I'll do this thing for you, Athania Dierá Steorra. When I'm done, you'll return to me what's mine." Takhbarre regarded Dierá, but he did not wait for her to respond. "This tunnel is for one of the old off-world gates. Disused now but still connected. If we continue along it, we'll come to the central thruway."

Dierá turned to G'rkyr. "You are the prince's champion and protector in this place. Nothing more. Don't forget that." Her words carried her annoyance. Her hold on G'rkyr seemed less than she thought. She wondered what report Jdes would give Nük T'nyr. Not that it would matter; nothing would matter soon. His disloyalty was nothing compared to what was ahead.

—

Martin settled into the holding area below Makhatar. In contrast to her viewing area filled with posh seats and wide aisles, this area was bare and little more than an expanse of washed stones. Gerhold was at his side. The other could do little else. Martin still held the leash of his collar and dared not release it.

Those in Makhatar's entourage seemed to speak their minds

plainly and openly. Now they complained loudly of this or that perceived slight. It was all about the view, the seats, the food, the drink. The pecking order applied here as well. Those at the top were the most vocal; each rung below, successively less so. Martin spoke only in quiet whispers and only when he was certain Makhatar's eye was not on him. He missed Tandy, the books they shared and the simpler life in hearth service.

His place in the order was unclear. It seemed he and Gerhold were part of a new sixth ring. It also could be that they simply had to establish themselves in the fifth ring—that of the Trykath pets of the first ring Drakón and titans.

The confusion was due in part to their sharing rooms with Trykathians, Alvs, and Dwëorgs alike. Clearly, the Alvs and Dwëorgs were a rung above the Trykathians. They were treated better, given more opportunity.

The crowds in the stands were dividing into cheering and jeering mobs. More and more poured into the seats and viewing areas. The stomping of their feet and clapping of their hands rose to a deafening roar. Wager papers traded hands. Vendors hawked their goods.

Makhatar's titans and Drakón placed many wagers. Most were against one they called the Soulless. There was no shortage of those in other high-placed viewing areas willing to take those bets. Attendants ran the wager slips back and forth by the handful.

Foodstuffs also were plentiful. Though all were castoffs from those higher up, it mattered not. A half-eaten cake discarded by a titan, a roasted shank tossed aside by a Drakón, or whatever else happened to be cast off was indeed better than anything he had ever found in Tandy's kitchens. He meant Tandy no disrespect, but her cooking could not compare.

Martin tripped over Gerhold as the Trykathians, Alvs, and Dwëorgs fought for viewing positions at Makhatar's feet. The sudden pain brought a strange numbness. He held his head against what he knew must be stinging pain, touched moistness, felt nothing.

All thought slowed. Martin realized he heard shouting and the banter of those around him, but he was outside it all. Makhatar projected her thoughts into his own. She called him to her side. "Stand ready," she told him. "The games begin."

CHAPTER TWENTY-THREE

Beneath a vaulted dome of stone, enveloped in absolute darkness, Yarr could not see the moons or suns, yet still felt them. In the same way he felt the wind. He could smell nothing save copper and ash, but he could imagine much more. The beating of his foe's heart, somewhere out there in the great arena. The clash of steel that came. The restless howling of tethered beasts with their mouths gaping in anticipation of the taste of flesh. Of his flesh.

He heard movement above his head, felt it beneath his feet. "Almost time," he told the others in Cikathian. "Be ready."

"They will come at us quickly, from all sides," someone else said. Yarr thought it was Sytek, one of the leaders of the Dwelmish group.

"No," he countered. "We are away from the commons. Our platform lifts at the masters' feet. Keep in the direction I face, put the suns behind you. Be warned, there are beasts near."

"They say ktoth are undying, that they can cross the distance of two double strides in one leap, that they have teeth as long as arms, that—"

"Ktoth are the least of our worries," Dhon said. He was a Fhurtroll and he did not fear death. "There's Empyrjurin out there or worse. No sense worrying about any of it. Others are doing exactly what we're doing—waiting."

"I don't care about any of them," another voice said.

"Do care," Yarr said. "Those with a cloth tied on the right are with us. Group and work together. Don't break and divide. Keeping together is our best hope."

Dhon moved to stand next to Yarr. "Fight as Yarr said, and you might live to see another day. They never reckoned on this. It will surprise."

What little there are of us, Yarr added in thought. His goal had been to convince many tens. They could have fought back; they might have been able to revolt. What he had been able to gather without fully revealing his aim was eighteen tens. Among them, Yarr, Xerc, and Dhon were the most experienced. If others changed sides, there would be more, but this he could not count on.

Yarr touched the coin medallion of Beqheth in his inside pocket. It seemed superstitious, this belief in her as the Mother of the Warrior, but who was he to judge otherwise. The Trojk Master believed. She had seen him through eight spectacles. With as much of the mob against him as for, he needed all the help he could get. He heard their boos and jeers. When once they had revered, calling him the Undying One, the Greatest of the Suprematics, they now loathed. They called him The Soulless One, The Accursed, The Blight, and on and on. There was no end to their curses. It worsened as more and more bet against him and lost. They wanted his death now as much as he wanted his life.

Yarr clutched at the spotted ktoth fur wrapped about his shoulders. It kept his muscles warm in the cold, damp pit. He heard the click of gears and the turning of pulleys. He lowered himself to lie on his back next to Dhon in the dirt. His thinness next to the troll's hulk was as a twig to a tree trunk. "You ready, Dhon?" he whispered.

"Auy, Yarr."

Yarr's Alvish eyes allowed him to see Dhon's huge, brutish face outlined against the darkness, and he heard in the voice a subtle dread. "This should not be our end. But like as not we cannot control our fate."

"You've been a good friend. If we're to die, then we die. It is the wish of the gods and damn them for it." Dhon cleared his throat and sang, very softly,

> *Gods under fire and heaven*
> *Fhur born, err I must go*
> *Grim, she shall keep me*
> *It is my own doing*
> *Her blanket I shall wear*
> *She shall keep me*
> *Should she wish it*
> *Under pall and thrall.*

Yarr felt ferocity build in his heart, for that was part of a warrior's tribute, but Fhurtrollen and not Alvish or Trykathian. The words walked the line between life and death. Both blessing and curse. They spoke of the duality of all things.

"I don't intend for us to die, Dhon. We'll use our numbers to our advantage."

"It'll surprise them, it will. I've always wanted to see the gods afeared."

The blocks overhead pulled back. Light crept into the pit. Yarr and Dhon spun around, moved to a crouch, waited. Yarr wondered about what could have been had he been able to unite all Supremators. He turned his eyes up to the light so his vision adjusted to the brightness, or he would be blinded like so many others at the start of it all.

The walls fell. The great stage was revealed. The gathered throng roared.

He determined his location. It was as expected; close to the masters so they could watch his death.

Across the stage, he saw clusters of other groups. And more.

All the platforms were raised.

All the beast pens were raised.

Seeing this, he wondered if it were possible to win the day. He did not lose hope.

Yarr clasped hands with Dhon, started to speak. That's when something hissed and roared, and Dhon cried out strangely. That's when the screaming and shouting started, and Yarr's group rose to their feet, surrounded by beasts, to face a thousand times their number swarming across the stage.

Yarr closed his eyes, and then jumped up with the rest of them. His hands gripped his spear, slung across his back was a great sword, and at his sides were daggers. He cast off his fur, wheeled around.

A lion-like rakor met him. It was black as death and big as any horse he had ever seen. He dug in with his spear, thrusting up and across. The rakor made the same sound as the one Yarr had been cloaked in, just louder and longer before it finally fell over.

Dhon was not as fortunate. He was set upon by three of the fierce eutoks—feral dogs with two heads. Yarr saw Dhon take the first, intervened before the second could land its brutal paws while Dhon dispatched the third.

"Gods!" Dhon shouted over the tumult and din. "What is this?"

"A wonder," Sytek replied. "I'm proud to die as part of this."

Yarr suspected it was the reenactment of some recent victory played out across the showground of the colosseum. He heard the watchers alternately cheer and jeer. It was eerie the way these sounds mixed in with the cries of great cats, the howls of dogs, and the baying of the creatures as yet unseen.

His hope was that he and his represented the victors. Somehow, though, he suspected otherwise. Someone among the masters had decided he was no longer useful, that it was past time for his death.

He rammed his spear home, felled one of the immense ktoth. He shouted, "No, never! Keep working together; live!"

The knot of the main battle moved to the center of the colosseum's vast stage. There Sytek met the glorious death he wished for at the hands of eutoks who tore him to shreds.

For a time Yarr lost track of Dhon and the others. Around them others were breaking and running. Separated, they had little chance. Even the strongest of them died wholesale, for living nightmares stalked alongside the ktoth, eutok, and rakor; nameless nightmares who knew only death and killing.

Together they fought on. Yarr's spear broke in the belly of some enormous grotesquerie. He broke out his sword. "Together, together!" he shouted desperately.

Somewhere close he heard the shriek of feral dogs. He slipped past a Fhurtroll hauling a pair of wounded Trykathians out of the main press of combat in the colosseum's center, to meet the pack of eutoks.

An eutok leapt at Yarr's chest and tore at him with its fangs while others went for his legs. He lashed out with his sword, cutting the first eutok nearly in half before turning on those at his legs. Finished, he wheeled around to find a group of Erlanders wielding spear and blade and forcing their way across the stage.

"Auy! Erland!" Yarr shouted.

Moving again, Yarr ducked the hilt of a S'h'dith warrior's sword as the warrior sought to bash in the side of his head. He whipped around, blade flying, and he caught the S'h'dith in the ribs. The warrior hissed and came on, thrusting himself up in a jumping attack. Yarr bobbed away, loosed his sword and felled the S'h'dith from the air.

One of the other S'h'dith warriors spun around with a dagger in his hand, releasing it in a quick thrust, but Yarr knocked it down with his own blade. He came back around to strike, but one of the Erlanders had already finished the S'h'dith. The man flashed Yarr a fierce smile. "Élvemere!" he called, his voice bright.

Yarr grinned at the man, lifting his bloodied sword. The man's eyes jumped up as something large tried to come down on Yarr from behind. It was enough of a warning to keep the beast from bowling Yarr over. He spun with this blade and shouted to the Erlanders in their own tongue, "Together, together! Rakor return!"

Together the Erlanders turned and plunged toward the rakor, forcing their way through the bunch of screaming beasts. Yarr joined them, as did others. One of the Fhurtrolls hacked out a rakor's throat with his saber and then, as blood fountained from the big cat, grasped the thick mane and cut the head from the body.

Another Fhurtroll, seeing this, let out a fierce cry, and Yarr was pleased to see it was Dhon. "Xerc? The others?" Yarr shouted.

"Broken most!" Dhon shouted. He used his sword to point out where some were as he fought on. "Xerc and his are closest. They hold their own. Sytek and his?"

"Gone most. Sytek too," Yarr replied. "Lost track of the others. Some few Dwelmish pushed past not long ago. These Erlanders broke through from the far side."

Yarr felt a presence behind him, turned to see Jdost. Jdost smiled a bloody smile. He was missing several teeth but was otherwise whole. Yarr feared treachery, but this feeling was fleeting. There was uncertainty in the gargant's eyes. The agreement between him and Jdost was a tenuous one; they had come to terms the day after Yarr bested the other on the training field. If the other Monsjurin guardians agreed, Jdost would fight with Yarr. Otherwise, the Monsjurin would fight for themselves.

Jdost raised Grekl, his blade. Yarr steeled himself. He had bested the gargant before and would do so again if needed. When Jdost kept his blade in the air, Yarr saw the gesture for what it was. A salute.

Yarr saluted the other openly, moved to Dhon's defense. The three, gargant, troll, and Alv, became a working trio. Their blades delivered death while they moved as one across the field.

CHAPTER TWENTY-FOUR

Dark thoughts took Yarr through a half toll. The great stage was littered with dead and dying. Side tunnels opened to admit hawkers, gravers, and setters. Hawkers cleared the stage of corpses; gravers ended the dying; setters carried props in and out. It was all part of the continuance, the cycle of the spectacle.

Yarr and his regrouped once again while the masters unleashed new terrors. It seemed that all around him were succumbing to the will of the mob, that he must follow shortly.

As if in answer to his darkest thoughts, the worst of the nightmares stood before him. It was three-headed and seven-legged, with hindquarters as tall as Jdost. Its mouths were nests for teeth and little else. It came at him snarling and howling.

The mob cheered its arrival; Yarr cursed it. He turned his eyes around the colosseum, watching those who watched him for a moment. They were Drakón, titan, and those who, like the Master of Keys, had won a part of their freedom yet would never truly be free. They came to the games through a series of way gates that carried them from places all across the hundred worlds.

Usually it did not bother him that they came to watch death. Today was different. They reveled in blood, in ways he had not seen before. It was as if they had lost themselves to their decadence. He felt nothing for them save perhaps pity. Death was his because it was all he had. They had lives, or at least he liked to believe they did. Death did not have to be their all, and yet it seemed death was.

Jdost and Dhon moved to help Yarr defend against the monstrosity; the beast wanted nothing of them. It kicked them back. Before they could break through, other foes found them.

Yarr defended wildly. Though he wielded his great sword with one hand at times, the weapon was meant for two-handed work. One weapon in two hands could not keep back such a beast, no matter how well wielded.

He felt death close in around him, fought to move out of the beast's kill box—the place where its three heads could all reach for him at once. He swung the blade in a wide arc, dropped his shoulder, rolled to avoid the gaping maws. He came back around, found another pair of waiting jaws. He stabbed, drew blood. He turned, thrust, drew blood.

The wounds brought rage and howls. His blood raced; his heart pounded.

The great stage was a mass of confusion and motion. Yarr caught glimpses of Dhon and Jdost as he defended. He knew the one direction he had to go to live. He spun, dashed around the hungry mouths, and fled toward open ground. He heard a roar of wind above him, and then suddenly the ground was rushing up to meet him. He screamed, tried to ensure he kept his grip on his sword, as he rolled and bumped along on his side and shoulder.

When he came to a stop, Yarr looked up to see three ravenous mouths diving toward him. He raked the ground, reached for his sword. Even as the beast came on, he thrust the blade up, struck a clean blow between two of the four front legs, and then dove frantically to one side.

The beast let out a sudden roar, clawing at the air. Moving too fast as it dropped to the ground, it skidded along and began to tumble end over end. Yarr heard a sharp crack, and the beast yelped.

Yarr regained his feet, looked around. It was a clean break to the neck of the first head, yet even as that head died, the other two sought to reach him.

Yarr drove in with his blade, thrusting deep into the middle head. His blade pierced one of the terrible eyes; he pushed in and up, ramming the blade in and out the other side. The creature howled piteously as it clawed the earth and sought to rise.

With the blade wedged, he switched to daggers. Taking one in each hand, Yarr went to dispatch the beast, but this death was something the mob did not want. They taunted and booed.

Yarr lifted his daggers and turned about on his heel until he faced the box seats, where he saw the ageless king, the consort, the son of Rnothen, and the Drakón prince. Their disappointment gave him power. He was the fly that buzzed and could not be swatted, the buzzer that bit and could not be caught. They could loathe him, but they could not kill him. Not in a fair fight anyway.

Her presence, though, took his power as much as Martin's had previously. She was unexpected. The sight of her broke him in ways he never imagined possible.

"My Dierá," he heard his second self say. Afterward, he heard a soft woman's voice calling to him, but it was not Dierá's. It was his mother's. "Hope for Élvemere," she said. His father seemed to agree, but his words were strange. "Windrunner," his father said. "The foals. One a colt now. Ride him. Dierá takes the other."

Second sight faded. Yarr knew only the colosseum. A dagger in each hand, he dispatched the third head even as the creature died of its wounds. He hacked off one of the heads, picked it up with both hands, and threw it. He spat, shouted out in Cikathian, "Élvemere lives forever!" With his point made, he went back to his bloody work.

On the other side of a struggling knot of Dwelmish, Yarr saw the huge Monsjurin Jdost, his sword lifting to clean the opposition out of his way. Yarr ran toward the gargant. Surely he could regroup with the gargant, but where was Dhon? Yarr did not see the Fhurtroll at first, and then he saw the other. Dhon was wounded, trying to regain his weapon; Jdost was defending alone against a pair of ktoth who were being marshaled by a S'h'dith.

Yarr reached Jdost at the same time as a large figure clad in well-worn leathers and helm. He slammed into the other. The other's shield rolled away, though he managed to keep a grip on his sword.

Yarr reached back with his daggers, preparing to strike. "Yarr, Yarr!" the other shouted. "It's me."

Yarr lowered his daggers. "Xerc? You live?"

Other Trykathians behind Xerc were pushing past. They swept by Jdost, began pushing the attackers back. Xerc replied, "For now."

Yarr reached up to grip the Trykathian's shoulder, and saw a ktoth sweeping down at him as he did. He turned the dagger in his hand around; the blade met flesh. He thrust with the dagger in his other hand, met flesh again. The ktoth crumpled at his feet.

Xerc blinked, pushed back his helmet. As he did, Yarr saw the other's wounds. He had been mauled about the head, and only the helmet kept everything together. He wondered how the other kept his feet. Trykathians were hearty, but Xerc must have been exceptionally so.

"Yarr," Xerc said. "It's been my honor—"

"Look out," Yarr shouted, and bulled into his friend, knocking over the large Trykathian and taking him down. One of the S'h'dith flashed past, his sword reaching out and catching Yarr in the shoulder.

Yarr felt the hot sting of the cut even as he struck back. His blows missed; Xerc's did not. Xerc took the other in the back. A clean strike. Yarr finished it, running the edge of his dagger from one side of the S'h'dith's throat to the other.

"I can't tell you how glad I am to see you," Yarr said. "I'd thought you were lost early on."

"Lost now," Xerc said, sinking to his knees. "It's been a good fight. Glory in death; death in glory."

Yarr helped steady his friend. "No death yet," he told the other, but as he said it, he saw the unmistakable shadow of a ktoth. He looked back as he spun around. Another S'h'dith was marshaling a group of ktoth, and he was joined by several companions. They were lining up for a thrust.

Yarr called out a warning. "Defend, ktoth! Meet the line!"

The ktoth hurtled toward them. The S'h'dith were only steps behind. Jdost and what remained of the Trykathian cavaliers met the line with a weak but still fighting Dhon amongst them. Yarr gripped his daggers and rushed forward.

He met a ktoth head on, moved left, and dug his blades into the side of the big cat's head. He leapt over the dying ktoth in a great swooshing arc that met the leading S'h'dith. His blows crushed the side of the scaly head.

Jdost lifted his blade and swung wildly at the next S'h'dith, as the other swerved to avoid him. Jodst missed; Yarr did not. The S'h'dith tumbled to the ground and was still.

Jdost looked over, pleased to see Yarr. "Dhon," he said. "He's not well."

"Xerc also," Yarr replied. "Only us soon."

Without warning a ktoth hurled itself at Yarr, plowing into his side and carrying him painfully to the dirt. Yarr lost one of his daggers, but swung at the ktoth with the other. The dagger glanced off, not even breaking the ktoth's hide.

The ktoth tore at Yarr with its fangs, drawing back just enough to come back at Yarr with its massive paws. It drove the air from his lungs.

Jdost came up behind the ktoth, grabbed it around the neck with both brawny arms. He squeezed, applying pressure until there was a loud crunch of bone and the big cat went limp.

Yarr got up just in time to see a S'h'dith coming for him. He turned, with a dagger clutched in his fist.

Jdost ducked rushing paws, blocked fangs, but went down on his backside, slipping in a bloody pool. He came back up with the sword he had lost moments before, scrambled ahead with Yarr. A bloodied Trykathian met them as they came on, but Yarr recognized the other as Xerc before striking. He shouted through the tumult and din, "Form up, behind!"

Yarr thought Xerc did as instructed, but he was not sure. The cavalier was haggard and had the look of death in his eyes. Yarr started moving again, staggering off into the wild melee of the colosseum. Soon after Yarr lost track of Xerc and Jdost, knew only the increasingly sluggish sweep of his dagger. His arm stopped when there were no more foes in front of him.

Exhausted, Yarr collapsed to the bloody field. He collected himself for a few handfuls of heartbeats, and then scavenged weapons for whatever came next. Others around him did the same. They rested, collected weapons, and prepared. Soon the few who remained were gathered in a knot. Yarr was pleased to see Dhon, Jdost, and Xerc among them, but they were not close.

Not far off, Yarr heard shrieks and howls. "What's happening?" He called out.

A Trykathian replied, "There, at the wall. Something emerges."

"From the tunnels?" Yarr shouted. "What?"

The Trykathian said, "Only Grim knows."

Whatever it was the mob had mixed feelings. Yarr heard calls of "Jurin, Jurin, Jurin!"

The knot of survivors fanned out into a loose ring. In their midst, Yarr saw him then, the Empyrjurin, wielding a sword as tall as Yarr himself. As the gargant approached, recognition came. Yarr knew it was G'rkyr even before Makhatar called out the other's arrival.

"Behold," Makhatar proclaimed in the language of the ageless. Martin and a Trykath Yarr did not recognize, chained at Makhatar's feet, were made to stand and shout out the same in Cikathian. "The personal champion of the Prince of Praxix. Best him and you will be freed from the games for all time."

Yarr knew then that he was truly cursed. In this there could be no victor, no victory. If he killed G'rkyr he would live, but he would lose Dierá's heart even if she told him otherwise.

CHAPTER TWENTY-FIVE

Deepening shadows on the field told Yarr the day was nearing its end. He marshaled the survivors, brought them into a tight knot in the center of the colosseum. They were not many in number, but those who breathed wore the cloth. It was victory regardless of what happened in the moments to come.

Side tunnels opened; hawkers and gravers entered. Yarr looked to Xerc, Dhon, and Jdost as he could. All three were injured; Xerc, the worst. In truth, there was little Yarr could do for any of them. Perhaps it was some trait of Trykathians that Yarr did not understand, but it seemed Xerc was dead and had only neglected to stop breathing. And yet Xerc gripped his great sword, much as Yarr gripped his own sword.

The gargant seemed in no hurry to make his way across the field. His armor with its spines and great horned helm seemed to displease him as much as it displeased Yarr. The onlookers loved the drama; alternately they applauded and jeered.

Yarr gave pointers to those with enough strength left to defend and fight. The armor would be difficult to pierce. He saw weaknesses only at the joints and neck. The face was open, but impossible for one of his stature to reach. When Yarr finished, Dhon said, "Beware the sweep of the blade. A reach half again as far as you think."

Jdost added, "The great sword is not his own. Not græsteel. Likely he won't be able to fire it."

"A pincer," Dhon said, opening and closing his large hand like a claw. "Jdost, Yarr and I go in direct. The rest, in two columns, come in from either side. Our best hope."

Yarr signaled his agreement, took a count of those who seemed able to fight. Xerc was not among them. It seemed his death had finally found him. "Go to your mother Beqheth," Yarr whispered as he closed Xerc's eyes. He turned sorrow to strength. He would have no regrets when this day was done. Either he would live to see the darkness of night or the darkness would take him. It would be as it would be.

Yarr brought his sword around as he awaited G'rkyr. Jdost and Dhon formed up those who could stand into two groups. None were unwounded. They were Dwelms, Erlanders, Kingdomers, Jurins, trolls, and Trykaths.

"I know this one," Yarr said quietly when Dhon and Jodst returned to his side. "I would count him a friend under other circumstances."

Jdost at first thought Yarr was making light of the situation, but then seemed to understand. "You, Yarr, are a contradiction," the Monsjurin said as he unslung his great widowmaker sword and donned his plumed helm. "The only Alv I know able to carry his ale and befriend us Jurin. Yrenil and the Wanderer would both be pleased to know you."

Yarr clasped forearms with Jdost and then with Dhon. "It's been an honor to know you."

"It's been my privilege," the Fhurtroll said as he readied a battleax.

Jdost took a wide stance. "And mine. You are forever welcome on R'hamtil. Simply speak my name to any of my order. They will know the truth of you."

Yarr flexed his tired legs, brought his sword to the ready. His Alvish eyes allowed him to see Dierá in perfect detail. Tears in her eyes matched the anguish on her face; whether for what was about to happen or for what he had become, he did not know. She sat at the feet of the fat Drakón prince who always bet against Yarr. Next to the prince was the son of Rnothen, the titan who came unendingly to see Yarr's death. He whispered in the Drakón king's ear while the king's consort on the king's other side muttered what must have been curses. Martin and an odd Trykath sat at the consort's feet.

One of the Erlanders let out an alarm. Yarr looked back in time to see dozens of Gnog pikers make running leaps from the beast exits. Jdost and Dhon turned, took positions at Yarr's sides, forming the triangle of a working trio. Each took a double step forward, readied for what came.

"Form two lines," Yarr shouted. "Meet the charge!"

Dhon blew out a breath. "A final toll."

Yarr turned his shoulder, prepared to receive G'rkyr's great sword. His position allowed him to see both the gargant's approach and the onrush of the Gnogs. "Not even that long. Jdost?"

"I'd wager not," Jdost said.

Down in the lines, one of the Dwelms cried out. Yarr saw a pike protruding from the man's chest. The man rolled back and then fell quietly to his side.

"His name is G'rkyr," Yarr said, "I know his brother, Zanük, as well."

An Erlander in the lines twisted around abruptly. He blinked a few times, put a hand to his throat where blood spouted. His eyes unfocused, he toppled to his side, a pike piercing his neck.

A foursome of Dwelms made running leaps, pushing into the oncoming Gnogs. They defended gallantly for a handful of beats, swords glistening in the light.

Dhon and Jdost took a single step back, closing ranks and preparing for pikes coming their way. Yarr brought his sword around, still waiting for G'rkyr to engage. "Begin, cowards," Yarr shouted in Cikathian. "Close already! We wait!"

The ranks closed; no more waiting. A second Erlander got stuck. A Gnog slammed a pike into the man's chest, below his ribs. The man let out a piercing cry, his blood suddenly a froth from his mouth.

A Trykath took a pike to the side of his head, even as he gave with his sword. The Trykath's head rolled back. He folded down and did not move again. The Gnog toppled to his side as well, the Trykath's sword piercing his belly.

A Dwelm crouched down behind his shield, tucking in his stocky legs and arms. A pike was rammed into the shield, pierced it, and went into the Dwelm's shoulder. The wound did not look life-threatening, but when the pike was ripped back out, the Dwelm went limp.

Yarr decided to close the distance between himself and G'rkyr. He took a step forward, then another. Jdost and Dhon turned and took two steps as well.

The main line was breaking now. A group of Kingdomers finished it by running. As soon as they turned to escape, they cried out almost as one and Yarr saw long, dark pikes impaling their chests, arms, and legs. They fell to the ground with shouts, some landing on top of each other.

A pair of Trykaths caught these Gnogs. Their swords met unprotected backsides. One of the Kingdomers tried to rise, but as soon as he did, a Gnog pushed a pike through him. A Trykath struck square to the Gnog's neck, pushed his blade in and through, much as the Gnog had just done with a pike. Blood fountained from the both sides of the Gnog's neck when the Trykath removed the blade.

In the stands the mob went wild, roaring and cheering. Jdost, Dhon, and Yarr chose this moment to launch. Jdost took the gargant from the right. Dhon, from the left. Yarr, from the front; three as one.

G'rkyr turned away Yarr's attack with a knee, stopped Jdost's sword with an arm, and met Dhon's ax with his sword. Sparks flew when the ax head met the sword's edge.

Jdost came back around with his blade as Yarr swept in. G'rkyr let out a shout and rolled forward, deflecting Jdost's blade into Yarr's attack. As the Monsjurin's blade swept across the front of the gargant's body, Yarr pulled back, went to go around, and came back in. Dhon spun, brought his ax sweeping across his body in a vicious arc at the gargant's head.

G'rkyr seemed to wait until the very last moment to move, and then he moved as fast as Yarr had ever seen anyone move. He thrust his mailed fist into Yarr's chest, nearly knocking the wind out of him, while at the same time twisting his body to one side so that the line of his body was beyond the descending sweep of the ax. The ax missed and slammed into the ground at G'rkyr's feet, where it kicked up a spray of dust and small rocks.

G'rkyr's sword was not still during this time. It was rising, coming around, then plunging into Jdost's side. Jdost's expression fell; a deep calm seemed to come over him. His stood stiffly, his mouth agape. The air whooshed out of his lungs as he let out a sudden, short groan. His fingers lost their grip on his sword, and then he folded down.

Yarr looked on in horror. G'rkyr tore the sword back out of Jdost's side and came around at Dhon, meeting the Fhurtroll's ax. The sound of clashing steel echoed throughout the colosseum. Blood on the gargant's blade sprayed outward. Yarr assessed, rushed in with his blade, and caught G'rkyr's next blow on it, hoping to give Dhon time to maneuver.

Yarr followed with four more blows, in a series of rapid thrusts, but the gargant deflected them all, despite Yarr's sheer speed and short, quick movements. Yarr was too close in and low to the ground to see the next strike, but he heard the resonant clash of steel on steel as Dhon's ax met G'rkyr's sword.

Yarr seized the opportunity to come in even closer, but as Yarr lashed out, G'rkyr brought the hilt of his sword down with both hands, bringing all his crushing might into Yarr's hands and then sweeping away Yarr's sword. The sword flew off somewhere behind him and he heard it land with a dull thud.

Yarr whirled around to get some distance between himself and the gargant. He did not reach for the dagger he held in reserve. Instead, he crouched and whirled around again with his hands wide and his legs bent and ready to leap. Dhon struck at G'rkyr's head, chest, and chest again. The gargant blocked each strike and then, with a sudden swiftness, his blade lashed out again. Dhon groaned, and the ax, pulled back with both hands over his head in preparation for a strike, fell to the dirt.

Even as Yarr leaped into the air, G'rkyr cut his blade across Dhon's middle, and Dhon cried out, "Grim take you!" But the voice was straggled and far away as Dhon staggered and fell. The Fhurtroll held in his guts with one hand while he groped the ground for his ax handle with the other. Yarr landed on G'rkyr's back at the same time the gargant tried to kick away Dhon's ax.

Yarr used his legs, locked them around the gargant's neck and squeezed with all his might. His hands he locked around the chin to keep the gargant's head where he wanted it.

Amidst the cheers, claps, and boot stomps, Yarr felt the world slow and shift around him. It was almost as if he was the only one alive. That everyone and everything else was beyond this time and place. That he was seeing through another's eyes. He heard a voice. It seemed very far away; it was screaming, screaming a single word: "Noooooooooooooooo!"

Yarr was falling, but it was the gargant who fell and not him. His legs and arms were fixed in place. He waited until the last, dropped and rolled as the gargant hit the ground, squarely on his back. The sharp strike was meant to crush Yarr, but instead pushed the wind out of the gargant.

Yarr closed his eyes against the dust spray, but did not pause. He drew his dagger, lunged forward from his knees. He found the gap between the gargant's armor and shoulder, shoved the dagger in. Using the blade dug into flesh as leverage, he swing himself up to the gargant's chest, then withdrew the blade and aimed it at the gargant's throat.

G'rkyr diverted the blow clumsily and Yarr drew a red line across the back of the gargant's hand. G'rkyr snarled, his face suddenly suffused with fire. He slammed his other hand into Yarr. Yarr felt the jolt of the blow in his chest and shoulders as he went sprawling.

Yarr hit the dirt on his side, rolled around, and jumped to his feet. His moves were almost catlike but the gargant was just as quick. The gargant stood over Yarr, both hands bunched into fists. He bore down, aiming to crush Yarr with a double blow. Yarr twisted his body, moved back, and the fists slid by.

Yarr delivered a counterstrike with his dagger, but not fast enough. G'rkyr dropped back to a guarded position, watching Yarr, his eyes wide, his face alive with fire. G'rkyr was still winded and wounded; he went to a knee, put a hand up as if to say stop, no more.

Yarr spun forward, deftly lunging, his dagger gliding toward the gargant. He slipped by the gargant's counter, stuck the blade into the knee joint of the gargant's armor, and twisted his body around the dagger until the hilt snapped off in his hand.

G'rkyr gasped, tried frantically to withdraw the blade. The blood made the blade too slippery to grip at first but he dug the blade out after a pair of heartbeats. Panting and groaning in pain, he looked up at Yarr, his face no longer lit with fire, his eyes questioning.

"Death knows you now, and you know her," Yarr said plainly as he jumped up and kicked the gargant in the face with both of his heavy boots. The move sent Yarr flying in one direction as the gargant fell back in the opposite direction.

Yarr rolled as he hit the ground and came back up on his feet. He stalked around the gargant until he was standing behind the other's head, then he lifted both arms in the air, hands balled into fists. "Your day's entertainment," he shouted in Cikathian as he awaited the judgement, "Blood and death! Damn you all!"

CHAPTER TWENTY-SIX

The twin suns of Cyvair began their decent as the mob roared and cheered Yarr's condemnation. Makhatar went to her feet. Reveling in the moment, she turned alternately left and right. Martin's expression said that he wanted no part of any of it, but he played to the crowd all the same while his Trykath counterpart stood mutely.

Yarr panted and sucked at the air. He scooped up a discarded sword and pike, drove them into the dirt at his feet. He was a bloody, dirty mess and bone tired. He stood ready, listened for turning wheels, the screech of the gates, the slide of the slats— sounds that meant new nightmares were coming his way. The mob had wanted his death only moments ago. Makhatar wanted his death still. If she wished it, he would breathe his last breath soon.

When Yarr turned to look for Dierá, sudden tears in his eyes matched her earlier tears. It seemed an age since he had cried, but it seemed all he could do. It was not anguish or sorrow or remorse that caused the tears, but absence and pity and grace. He was devastated to find Dierá absent; he pitied the mob and their hatred; and yet he had found grace. "Élvemere lives," he whispered to his father and mother, for he felt their presence as strongly as he had ever in life, "if only as a dream in my dying heart."

Yarr turned calm, sympathetic eyes to Makhatar. He pitied her most of all. Her life was the smaller one. Truly. She was the thing to be studied and pitied. The wealth of the Hundred Worlds was hers, and yet she was so self-loathing and jaded she could not find joy in any of it. She felt the weight of the worlds every day and had lived less in her centuries of freedom than he had lived in a hundred years in captivity; she was the slave and not he. He could let go of this life and find freedom. She would never be free, not in this life or in the next.

Yarr was about to shake his fists in the air, but sank to his knees instead for he felt them then. The soft presence and the mighty one; both demanding his attention.

"You just don't know when to die properly, do you, Alv?" The sharp voice in his mind was unmistakable; it was Makhatar's.

"Be strong," Yarr said as he swept up the sword from the dirt. He turned his eyes to Dierá among the hawkers and gravers, answering her soft call to him as he did so. "The Merciless One knows you and will welcome you."

Yarr turned calm, sympathetic eyes to Makhatar. Martin spoke her judgment and the mob agreed. "Death for the Jurin."

"Take as you can," Yarr shouted in Cikathian. "Mercy is what I will deliver." He made a spectacle of sweeping his sword, delivering it to the dirt beside a fallen Monsjurin, lunging at a fallen Fhurtroll. He leapt into the air, landed on top of the fallen Empyrjurin.

As he stalked across the gargant's chest, he saw his mother open his arms to him. He smiled, saw Dierá look to those he had pointed out, and then he struck, plunging in the blade, delivering the blow to the heart between armor and ribs.

The deed done. He fell down to his backside, smiling still. Blood flowed from the wound delivered by his own hand and frothed from his own mouth. The twin suns gave the last of their light as he took in the last of his breaths, and he went to the darkness unafraid, knowing there was yet light and hope.

He had dared to dream a dream of Élvemere. It was the one true thing he could believe in. He was humbled and blessed that something so precious had been given to his care. "Please, please, please, forgive me," he said in Alvish. "I dared dream, and when Élvemere could not live otherwise, I gave what left I had."

Yarr no longer saw the waking world. Instead, his second self saw the flat, open grasslands of his beloved homeland where Windrunner's son waited for him. He climbed onto the young stallion's back and raced with the winds across the sweeping plains to the great forest. Soon he was standing outside his father's pavilion of rich blue silks and yellow satins.

"Join us," said his father, calling out from within the pavilion.

"Yes, please. Hurry now," his mother said.

Yarr put haste to his step. "Pritish," he said in greeting as he entered.

"Salus, salut," his father replied.

"Sit," his mother said. She poured a steaming cup of blue elder juice and set it before him. "Drink this, find peace. There is hope. Without doubt, you are the Light of Élvemere." She looked to her husband. "Our walk now?"

Yarr's father nodded, took her hand, and she in turn took Yarr's. The three left the pavilion and began walking. Windrunner and his kin followed.

Yarr had been drifting for so long, but now he was home. He could breathe again. All his troubles and fears dissolved. He believed; all was possible. He could dare to lose himself completely now, and did.

"Goodbye," he said to Dierá. Her face and lips before his mind's eye were the answers at the end of the light. She was faithful and strong. She would cast him gently to the night and help him forgive the cruelty of this day. "Don't worry. Time will heal all. Everything will come around and one day Élvemere will live. No matter what, it was worth the cost."

But these words were not Yarr's, they were Dierá's, and he realized he had returned to the waking world. He lived, breathed, and Dierá cradled him in her arms. "Forgive me," she said, the hungry white power of life still flowing from her mouth to his, "I could not bear to live without you."

The mob was in an uproar. Rioting began. Drakón and titans were being escorted away to safety by S'h'dith warriors. The magi were frantically erecting perimeters of magic to hold back the crowds. Trykaths were pouring into the stadium from every side tunnel. The skies over the stadium were alive with flyers and buzzers of many sorts.

Dhon, Jdost, and G'rkyr lived. They were circling protectively, holding back the Gnogs and Trykaths. Makhatar was furious, screaming as she rode a wave of power in a crescendo from the stands to the stadium floor. The king, the titan, and the fat prince were at her side.

"You?" Makhatar screamed. "How dare you!"

Dierá answered, "I am Athania Dierá Steorra of the Élvemere and I dare all."

Makhatar clawed at Dierá. The titan and the Drakón prince interceded before she could land her blows. "These will best serve in life, not death," the titan said. "Retribution in service," the prince said. "Subscribe them in the war against the Jurin armies."

Makhatar pulled back, thought better of it, and came back round with her claws. Only the king's words stopped her from striking. "No," he said plainly and firmly.

The prince spoke into the king's ear. "Surely they've proven themselves. Let them bring death to our enemies."

The king waived the prince back, waved back Makhatar's blind outrage. "Bind them as need be. Life service in the corps. No one will broach disapproval in this."

And so, Yarr's new life in service to the corps began.

About the Author

Robert Stanek is the bestselling author of more than 100 books for young people and adults. He lives with his wife and children in the Pacific Northwest in the United States, and is intensely fascinated with our natural world. He loves the outdoors and frequently takes his family on short trips to see the natural wonders of the Pacific Northwest.

Learn more at www.robertstanek.com

Enter the world of Ruin Mist
www.ruinmistmovie.com

ROBERT STANEK
BATTLE for RUIN MIST
BETRAYAL
A DAUGHTER OF KINGS
COMIC #1

Enter the other realm now and see what she sees. Dark dreams disturb her sleep. She is a daughter of kings about to be dealt fate's darkest hand. Her name is Delinna Alder.
Strange sounds awake her. Frightened, she sits up and looks around her room. She makes deep noises in her throat, can you hear them?
Hello? Hello!
She puts a hand to her head, her eyes wide with terror. In her mind's eye she sees a phantom surrounded by tendrils of lightning and flame. It is magic. Darkness to those who believe the ancient texts; light to those who can see beyond prejudice and fear.

It is him.

The one they call the Watcher, returned from afar. But she does not know that as she screams. She sees only the phantom emerging from shadows.

Shadows left behind, hood lowered, the face is revealed. She knows him. He is Xith, a shaman of the northern reaches and the last of the watchers. To some, he is an impish gnome. To her, he is salvation.

You found it at last?

He doesn't answer. His face is grim; his mood, ever darker. It is a strange hour to intrude on a princess's sleep. A strange hour to wake a daughter of kings.

You startle me awake and say nothing?

If the Watcher seems familiar to you, that's as may be. Like the Keepers, Watchers have been seen across time. They are both within time and outside its bounds.

Smell her fear as he reveals it. She knows immediately that it is one of the four—an Orb of Power fashioned by Dnyarr, the last great Elf King of Greye. The orb is what the Watcher has been seeking; why he has arrived at such an odd hour.

If Keepers are masters of lore, dream and shadow, Watchers are masters of voice, magic and illusion. His command can be her will. Her fear to this will be as wind to water.

He shows it to her.

Touch it!

I mustn't!

You must!

She doesn't want to, but it beckons to her. She must touch it. How could she do otherwise? And yet she is able to refuse its pull if only for a few beats of her heart. The toll will tell true though. It will. This I can say for sure.

Please, no.

Answer its call. Take it now. Both hands. No fear.

It responds to her touch, exploding to life as legend says it must, for she is a daughter of kings. It feeds on her earliest memories first, ripping them from her and leaving her gasping before tearing through all the days of her young life. It knows her now as even she does not yet know herself.
Hungry still. It looks for more; it reaches out to him. He holds the power back, keeps it from consuming him and her.
Stop! No more!
How? Is it even possible? It wants so much more. It hungers.
It wants ME-E-E!
We've only begun. The orb gives as much as it takes. You must ask it to give back.
The keys, you have them. Don't think, do, and it will respond.
Then give yourself to it!
The Watcher commands and Delinna gives. She hopes it has the answers she's long sought, but at what cost? Her salvation? Her damnation? There's always a cost. Sometimes, a cost in flesh. Other times, a cost far greater for just as the ages cut across time, so does the power of the orb. It knows no bounds and no one person can truly contain its power.
But will it tell her who lives and who dies? These are the answers long sought and the reasons for the Watcher's long journeys across dark lands. True enough, death and sorrow have been foretold, but can these things be undone before they are done? Will the Alders end truly bring down the Kingdoms of Men?
The One True Path has many turnings and a woman's quest must begin with a girl's decisions. But who can be saved and who must be lost? Difficult choices for anyone. For one as young as she, choices that will haunt the days of her life.

See her, know her enduring sadness. A child now, a sister, but not a child in this second sight. One of many Alders who will die if the foretold comes to be.
She leaves the loneliness of Imtal in search of a much loved sibling. It is this search that will ensure her survival and perhaps that of her people. She is key as much as coffer.
Take control of the orb or it will control you.
Do as I command. Tell it to show you who must live.
Exert your will. Demand release. Command!
Yes, find control, focus. That's it now. We must be sure. We must know more.
It wants too much. Its touch is agony. The pain!
Please, make it stop. Let me find release. I can't. No more!
It wants. I feel it devouring all that I am.
Her, and them, and him. They are the ones I see most clearly.
See the two, know their determination. They are Elves of the Reaches, not seen in the Lands of Men for a thousand years. Of the two, one will be lost and the other saved, and yet both must live. How can this be so?
They leave Leklorall, City of Elves, in search of hope, but will find betrayal instead of brotherhood. Men and elves are enemies as it has ever been since the War of Blood.
Give me release. P-l-e-e-a-s-e! I beg you take it from me.
No more, no more! I want none of it. It hungers; I can't control it.
Don't cry, hold in the pain. Almost done... Yes, we are, and then rest.
Rest comes, a deep peace. Hold on only now—yes, there... That's it. Pass it willingly now.
See the boy, child of her loins, know his terror. See him meet his death in the eyes of the great beast. It is a shifter. The shifters have a part. Yes, they do. Terrible and dark.

Good, good. That's it. A careful focusing now.
Is it over? Will it ever be over? Can it ever be over?
You've done well. Now command it! Pass your power to me for safekeeping.
You are safer now without this burden. Power as this was not meant for your hands. The line may be kept and it may be Adrina saved. There is hope. The shifters will hunt me now.
Would that she were that fortunate. It hunts by instinct. Quickly, efficiently, dispassionately. It will find a way to feel her touch again. To make her tremble, to know her fear, to grasp her innocence. He knows all this, but says nothing for now. The knowledge would consume her as surely as it wants to consume her even now.
For all?
I want nothing of gifts or powers. I want only peace and quiet. Rest.
The Keeper comes, accept his gift willingly.
The Watcher leaves her to her peace and quiet, to her rest. But can you smell it? Not the sweat of her labors, but the fear. It has returned unasked for. She sees the things the orb has shown her, feels the length of the chain wrapping the ball of the world.
Even at this young age, she senses her destiny, knows its impossible weight and measure.

9 781575 450971